CHAMPION

& JEWBOY

TWO NOVELLAS

Bruce H. Siegel

ILLUSTRATIONS BY SPARK

ALEF DESIGN GROUP

These stories are dedicated
to the memory of my father,
James E. Siegel

יַעֲקֹב אֵלִיָּהוּ בֶּן שְׁמוּאֵל עָיֵיה

who still teaches
and from whom I still learn.

LIBRARY OF CONGRESS CATALOGING-IN-PUBLICATION DATA
Siegel, Bruce H.
    Champion ; & Jewboy / Bruce Siegel ; illustrations by Spark.
        p.   cm.
    Summary: Two stories about Jews, the first relating a boy's exploration of his
grandfather's career as a boxer in pre-war Germany, and the second about a white-
supremacist youth's discovery of the horrors Jews have suffered throughout history
because of antisemitism.
    ISBN 1-881283-11-9 : $6.95
    1. Jews—History—Juvenile fiction. [2. Jews—History—Fiction.
2. Antisemitism—Fiction 3. Grandfathers—Fiction. 4. Holocaust, Jewish (1939-
1945—Fiction. 5. Germany—History—Fiction.]
I. Spark, ill. II. Title. III. Title: Jewboy. IV. Title: Champion & Jewboy. V. Title:
Champion and Jewboy.
    PZ7.S575Ch   1995
    [Fic]—dc20   94-44172
                                                                                              CIP
                                                                                               AC
ISBN# 1–881283–11–9
Champion & Jewboy. Copyright © 1996 Bruce H. Siegel
Illustrations Copyright © 1996 Spark
Published by Alef Design Group

ALEF DESIGN GROUP • 4423 FRUITLAND AVENUE, LOS ANGELES, CA 90058
(800) 845–0662 • (213) 582-1200 • (213) 585–0327 FAX

MANUFACTURED IN THE UNITED STATES OF AMERICA

CHAMPION

I

At Grampa Ben's funeral, I think the worst thing (aside from the obvious) was the fact that it was a beautiful day--sunny, warm and clear. Beautiful days and funerals go together like Hershey Bars and sardines.

Since Grampa lived only a couple of miles from us, the rabbi from our synagogue officiated, and I was prepared not to like anything he said. Grampa never went to *shul* and the rabbi hardly knew him, so I was prepared for a one-size-fits-all eulogy. "We are gathered here today to honor *(insert name here)*..." Lots of lofty words, none of which had anything to do with Benjamin Rendsberg or the life he'd just completed.

Surprisingly, the rabbi was eloquent but restrained, sincere but not gushy. He mentioned Grampa's early years in Germany, his prowess as an athlete, his emigration to America just before Hell and Hitler swallowed up Europe's Jews, his success in business, and the family that was the center of his universe. He'd always supported Israel and bought a big Israel Bond every Yom Kippur (but never showed up for Kol Nidre). I guess I'm most thankful that instead of praising my grandfather as being a pious Jew (which he wasn't), the rabbi called him an exceptional human being (which he was). I think Grampa Ben would've liked that.

About fifty people showed up for the funeral and made the five mile trek to the cemetery for the burial. Aside from the family, the people in attendance were mostly Dad's friends, and associates and clients from his law office. A few of Mom's friends came, too. Grampa had outlived all his cronies but one, Mr. Klemmer, who, in a natty black suit and derby hat, stood off to one side, away from the crowd.

The rabbi finished the service, shoveled three spadefuls of earth into the grave, and invited the family to do the same. We all took our turn: Dad, his two sisters, and the four (of Grampa's seven) grandchildren who'd made it to the funeral. I went last, not only because at sixteen I was the youngest of the grandchildren, but because I wanted to hand the shovel to Mr. Klemmer. Even though he wasn't Jewish, I wanted him to participate.

Mr. Klemmer and Grampa had grown up together in Germany and had emigrated within a couple of years of each other. They had been like unjoined Siamese twins since they were kids. Each had been the other's shadow. They had both been amateur boxing champions (Grampa as a lightweight, Mr. Klemmer as a street-tough middleweight). After they had both taken up residence here in Massachusetts with their respective houses not 3/4 of a mile from each other, they had gotten together at least twice a week for decades to play two-handed pinochle, shoot pool or

talk boxing, and argue. When the two of them would play pool in our basement rec room, the rest of us knew enough to stay clear.

Three days before Grampa died, the two of them were downstairs playing eight-ball. After an hour or so, the conversation descended into all-too-familiar territory.

"Why don't you shoot the one-ball?" Grampa had said.

"From you I don't need advice," said Mr. Klemmer drawing a bead on the three.

"You shoot the one and you'll have position on the four."

"I'll make my own shot, thank you very much."

"Take the three and where will you go?"

"Off the cushion and over here for the one. Then the four. Leave me alone."

"Why bother with the cushion? Take the one."

"Do I talk when it's your turn?"

"Does a bird have wings?"

Mr. Klemmer tossed his cue onto the table, knocking a number of the balls around. "That's it. When you're better than me, *then* you can tell me what to do."

"I'm not telling, I'm suggesting."

"You suggest too much."

"That's because you need suggesting."

"The hell you say."

"The hell YOU say."

"No, the hell YOU say. I've had enough of this." Mr. Klemmer stormed over to the cue rack, replaced his cue, grabbed his jacket, and headed for the stairs. "Every time I'm winning you pull this garbage. You can't beat me so you try to annoy me. I know you from way back, Binny. Playing with the head. It's always playing with the head, isn't it. You think I'm like that dumb *shlub* from Bremen? Huh?"

"I don't know what you're talking about."

"The hell you don't."

"THE HELL I DO!"

"Idiot."

"Moron. Get outta my house."

"It's not your house, and I wouldn't stay if you begged me."

"I wouldn't let you stay if you paid me."

Mr. Klemmer stomped up the steps into the kitchen muttering in German. I'd just come home from school and was eating a sandwich and reading the new *Time* magazine. Mom was working on dinner. Mr. Klemmer lowered his thermostat slightly for our benefit.

"Excuse me, I have to go home."

"Bye," Mom and I said without bothering to look up from what we were doing. We'd seen this show a million times. In my head I counted down, "…three…two…ONE."

"Hey," Grampa's voice bellowed from downstairs, right on schedule. "Next Thursday?"

"Friday," Mr. Klemmer snapped back as he walked out the kitchen door. "I've got a doctor's appointment."

It was to be their last exchange, and I'm sure that as Mr. Klemmer pushed some earth into the hole, the words were playing and replaying in his head like a broken record. With all their screaming and fighting, I doubt two lovers could have cared about or needed each other more. The night after Grampa died, I was surprised that Dan Rather didn't mention them on the evening news.

After the funeral, everyone came back to the house for bagels, whitefish and eggs. Dad and his sisters sat on low corrugated cardboard boxes provided by the funeral home, and quietly accepted condolences.

Mr. Klemmer didn't eat anything. He sat (again off to the side) stiffly upright in his expensive but tasteful suit (he'd owned a menswear store for years, and always dressed the part), and stared through glassy eyes. Seeing him there, as much in mourning as any member of our family, I thought he looked out of place, a vestige of a lost time when honor, dignity, and loyalty were judged more important than money, position and power.

Convention had been the cornerstone of Mr. Klemmer's (and Grampa's) life. Certain things were to be done, and they were to be done a certain way. You always stood, held the door, and tipped your hat when a lady walked by. You always wore a long-sleeve shirt with the collar buttoned, even on the hottest of days. You always deferred to the doctor. You always minded your own business, and respected other people's privacy. You never gloated over a fallen adversary, and you never talked about serious family problems (yours or anybody else's) with anyone but your closest friend. You paid all your debts, monetary and otherwise, on time and in full. You never borrowed money from a friend, or sold anything to family. And if you *did* loan money to a relative, you never asked for repayment, no matter how overdue it was. You married once and for life, occasionally spanked the children, and never raised a hand to your wife.

And when someone died, even if you hadn't liked him, you said only good (or at least neutral) things about him, not just to his family, but to anyone who asked. When a neighbor of his died, the worst thing I ever heard Grampa say about the man was "We didn't always see eye to eye…," even though the two of them had been at each other's throats for years and the guy had once bounced a check in one of Grampa's drugstores.

I realized that with Grampa gone, Mr. Klemmer was the last link to a time that would soon exist only in books. I also knew that my knowledge of Grampa's

11

early years was awfully meager, and that Mr. Klemmer was the only source of information left to me. Dad had told me stories about how Grampa would have gone to the 1936 Olympics, but that Jews weren't allowed on the German team. How his family had shipped him to America, hoping he could get enough money together for tickets and visas for his parents, brothers and sisters, and any other relatives he could save before the doors out of Germany were closed and sealed. How, with the money amassed and the papers in order, Grampa had tried frantically and unsuccessfully to contact his family. Neighbors back in Nuremberg told him, after the war, how the Rendsbergs and all the other Jewish families in the area had been loaded into open trucks one morning and had disappeared.

These stories I knew. But there were big gaps. How come the family had sent *him* over to arrange passage and not one of his older, worldlier, wealthier brothers? Why, after a fairly religious upbringing, did he seem to have nothing but contempt for Judaism? Why, after a stellar career as an amateur fighter, didn't Grampa turn pro when he came to America and make some really good money? And where was the money he had made from the string of pharmacies he'd built, managed, and sold for mega-bucks (we assumed) to a large marketing conglomerate?

I walked across the room, and sat down next to Mr. Klemmer.

"How you doing?' he said without turning his head.

"Okay, I guess."

He took a deep breath. "Do you know how fast he was, your grandfather?"

"You mean when he was boxing?"

Mr. Klemmer nodded slightly. "We would make jokes about how Binny's hands were so fast his shadow couldn't keep up."

I smiled. Only Mr. Klemmer ever called him Binny. It was short for Binyamin, Grampa's real name.

"I knew all his moves, all his tricks. But when we sparred, I could never catch him. It was like trying to catch smoke."

Mr. Klemmer looked me in the eye. "He would have been Olympic champion, you know. No amateur in the world could touch him."

"I know. Dad told me how the Nazis wouldn't let him on the team."

Mr. Klemmer's eyebrows merged in a frown. "Is that what he told you, your father? That the Nazis wouldn't let Binny fight?"

"Something like that, yeah. Isn't that what happened?"

Mr. Klemmer looked away from me.

"No."

I was stunned. The tale of Grampa Ben and the Nazis who wouldn't let a Jew represent their country had been a staple of my bedtime lore for as long as Dad had told me stories. "So what really happened?"

Mr. Klemmer said nothing. There was a long, awkward lull.

"I really blew it," I finally said, changing the subject.

"What do you mean?"

"There were so many things I wanted to ask him about his life. But I never did, because I figured there would always be a later." I pulled a fresh Kleenex from my pocket and used it. "There are things I need to know about him, Mr. Klemmer, not just boxing stuff. And you're the only person who knows. I knew my grandfather as a grandfather. That's it. I need to know about him as a man. I need to know before…"

I hit the brakes.

"Before I join him?" Mr. Klemmer said.

I hung my head, embarrassed.

Mr. Klemmer slowly stood up. "Wait here," he said as he went to the closet to retrieve his hat. I watched him lift it down from the shelf, examine it, and gently blow a fleck of dust from the crown. Hat in hand (he'd never put his hat on indoors), he walked back to my seat. I tried to stand but he laid a heavy hand on my shoulder which I couldn't have budged if I'd wanted to, and whispered in my ear.

"Do you know who Benny Leonard was?"

I shook my head no.

"I can tell you what you want to know about your grandfather. But it won't mean anything to you until you learn about Benny Leonard, who he was, what he did, and what he represented. When you find all that out, come see me and we'll talk, you and I. Once you know how big a part he played in my friend Binny's life, then your questions will have answers."

The powerful hand patted me on the shoulder, and he walked away for a final word with my father. As I watched, it was impossible to say who was consoling whom.

II

February, 1931. The Nuremberg Boxhalle and Gymnasium. Three boxing rings, ten light and heavy punching bags, the dense smell of sweat, mildew and dreams, the sound of skipping ropes flicking under feet. Racks of dumbbells, medicine balls, mats, and pulleys. A row of mirrors on one long wall and on another, an enormous sign. FEAR, it says in huge block letters. LOSERS DENY IT. WINNERS CONFRONT IT. CHAMPIONS DEFEAT IT.

There was an incredible upsurge of interest in boxing for two reasons. First, the Olympics Games are coming to Berlin in 1936. And second, Max Schmeling is the Heavyweight Champion of the World.

In June of 1930, Max challenged Jack Sharkey, an American, for the title. For three and a half rounds Sharkey pummeled Max severely and seemed assured of an easy win, when a low blow caught Max in the groin, and he collapsed in a heap, rolling on the canvas in agony. He was carried back to his corner and declared "'winner by foul" and new Heavyweight Champion of the World. Upon his return to Germany with his somewhat tarnished crown, boxhalles like the one in Nuremberg began to appear across the country and fill with boys hungry to be the next Max.

The undersized thirteen-year-old leaning against a wall, clutching a violin case was one of them.

"What do you want?" Herr Schiller the Head Trainer had barked at him.

"Boxing lessons."

"What a surprise. Eight marks a week, towel and locker fee two marks extra per month. Group lessons Wednesday and Saturday. Private lessons are extra. Additional group lessons are extra. You got shoes?"

"Yes."

"Good. Shoe rental is extra. Soap is extra."

"Do you charge extra for air?"

Herr Schiller's recitation stopped short.

"What?"

"You charge extra for everything else. I was curious if the air was free."

The trainer scowled menacingly. "Beat it, you little...what did you say your name was?"

"Rendsberg."

"Listen, Rendsberg, take your violin and go home. Come back when you've gained some weight and learned some manners."

"I'm ready now," said the kid, opening the violin case. Inside were a T-shirt, shorts, socks, sneakers and a towel.

Herr Schiller did some quick mental permutations.

"You're supposed to be at a music lesson aren't you?"

"I have the money."

"That's not the point, kid. No offense, but your people aren't athletes. They play the violin. They're doctors and lawyers. Jews and gyms don't go together."

"Don't you think you could teach me?"

Herr Schiller drew in and let out a long breath.

"All right, Rendsberg. Put your sneakers on and get into ring #2."

"What about the rest of my clothes."

"Don't worry. This won't take long."

Binyamin Rendsberg climbed into a ring for the first time. An assistant trainer laced him into a couple of 16 ounce gloves that were the size of pillows and a head-guard that was at least two sizes too big. A rubber mouthpiece that made him gag was inserted between his teeth. Across the ring, Herr Schiller was lacing the gloves of a boy who was not only big but, with the head-gear low over his eyes, looked to be only a few evolution-ary steps removed from his Neanderthal ancestors. Rendsberg thought about his violin lesson.

Herr Schiller walked to the center of the ring. "All right," he called out to the thirty or so boys gathered at ringside. "To draw the guard down, jab to the head, jab to the body, shoulder feint another body jab and right cross over the top. Paul and Rendsberg here will demonstrate." He motioned them together. "Touch gloves." They did. "Rendsberg, keep your guard up. Take it easy, Paul. Set it up with the left jab only. BOX!"

The bigger boy snapped out a high jab, but Binny's head was buried behind his gloves. The next jab went between Binny's elbows and thudded against his skinny chest, knocking him back a step.

"Keep your hands up, Rendsberg," called Herr Schiller. "All right, Paul."

Paul's shoulder dipped as if he were about to throw another body blow. Binny's hands dropped to protect his stomach, and a whistling right sailed out of nowhere, catching him high on the forehead and dropping him on the seat of his pants.

"You see," said Herr Schiller to the class. "Feint with the shoulder, cross over with the right. You all right, Rendsberg?" Binny nodded as he clambered awkwardly to his feet. "Good. Again. Double up this time, Paul. Mix up your pattern."

The bigger boy moved in and pumped two jabs at Binny's head. The gloves were becoming heavy, and Binny was having difficulty protecting his face. Two jabs to the body. Two more to the head. The punches weren't hard, but Binny found it exasperating that his opponent could keep him this befuddled using only one hand. Paul jabbed to the body, feinted a second, threw the right and sent Binny sprawling again.

"That's enough, Paul. Peter and Gunther, you're the next pair."

"NO!"

Herr Schiller turned around. Binny, using the ropes to haul himself upright, was on wobbly legs, a trickle of blood running from his nose. He was furious, not because he'd been knocked down, but because he'd been suckered twice by the same move. He spit out his mouthpiece. "Once more."

"That's enough, Rendsberg. Leave the ring."

"ONCE MORE!"

Herr Schiller put his arm on Binny's shoulder and said in a low voice, "I admire your courage. I'm admitting you to our program starting next week."

"I don't care." He gestured across the ring to Paul who was removing his headguard. "I want him to try that again."

"Suit yourself." Herr Schiller was the absolute monarch of his domain. No one, much less a violin-toting Jew who just walked through the door was going to raise his voice like this. The trainer walked to Paul's corner, helped him replace his headgear, and said "Put him down. Hard."

Paul bit down squarely on his mouthpiece and moved in, jabbing his left at Binny's head and chest almost at

19

will. Paul didn't like any of it. This Rendsberg kid was inexperienced, exhausted, and outweighed by at least twenty pounds. But Herr Schiller had given an order, and the order would be carried out.

Paul's shoulder hitched, Binny's hands dropped instinctively, and the right was launched. But this time, at some point during the quarter of a second it took for the punch to reach its target, Binny took a short stutter-step backward, and the punch whizzed past his ear and over his shoulder carrying Paul into the ropes.

"That's enough," Herr Schiller said stepping quickly between the boys. Paul had come off the ropes with embarrassment on his face and mayhem in his eyes. "That's enough. Now hit the showers, both of you."

Paul left the ring, but Herr Schiller held onto Binny's arm. "4:00 Wednesday," he said. "Be here on time, or don't bother coming. A fighter needs discipline, and that starts with punctuality." He wiped Binny's bloody nose with a towel. "Go get cleaned up. And try to think of a creative excuse to give your parents for why you missed your violin lesson."

Paul was sitting on a bench in the locker room when Binny walked in. They unsmilingly eyed each other until Paul stood up and offered his hand.

"I'm Paul Klemmer."

"Binyamin Rendsberg," said Binny taking the hand.

"What kind of a name is Binyamin?"

"Jewish. Is that a problem?"

"Nope." Paul headed back to his locker. "No hard feelings?" he called over his shoulder.

"No hard feelings."

"Good. Now tell me how you did that. How'd you make me miss?"

Binny shrugged. "I don't know. I really don't."

He was telling the truth.

III

The shiva period of mourning is supposed to be seven days, but Dad said four days was enough seeing as how we weren't orthodox and seeing as how Grampa would've thought spending such a large amount of time being isolated and feeling miserable was stupid. "Ritual is rigmarole," I heard him say to Dad once. "It takes no brains to walk the same rut over and over again."

"Come off it, Pop," Dad had responded calmly. "Your whole life is a ritual. Always has been."

"What are you talking about?"

"You spend the same amount of time doing the same things with the same people every week, every year."

"That doesn't make it smart," Grampa had responded gruffly.

"No, but it's comfortable."

"You want comfort, put on warm socks."

"And it's familiar."

"So's a rerun on TV. Who needs it?"

"You do. Everybody does. When you used to go to the gym, didn't you follow a ritual? Stretching, then running, then working the speed bag, then sparring then…?"

"That was different."

"Why?"

"Because," he said gently jabbing Dad's chest with an index finger, "that's how you produced a good fighter. When you go to shul and you read the same prayers every week, what do you produce? Boredom! Wasted time! A big fat nothing."

"I disagree. There's a feeling of peace. A sense of community. The knowledge that I'm standing alongside my…OUR ancestors in a chain that goes back almost 40 centuries. That's not nothing."

"I'm sorry, Lou, I'm old and that's the way I feel."

"So you're not against rituals in general, just religious ones, is that it?"

"Stop playing lawyer, Mr. Lawyer. I'm not going to argue with you in your house."

Dad smiled. "You want to go outside?"

"Don't be a smart guy," he chided sarcastically as he stood up from the kitchen table. "I'm gonna see what the kids are doing." Which, Dad knew, really meant "I'm leaving before I get beat up even more." A good fighter never ignores the strategic value of organized retreat.

Anyway, Dad said four days of shiva was enough, and everybody concurred.

The day after shiva we went to Grampa's house to sort through his possessions. I dreaded going there, but it wasn't too bad. With Grampa gone, most of his things were just things. Pictures were special, though. And his clothes. He'd lived simply in this little house for as long as I could remember, and there was little clutter.

"If there's anything here you want, let me know," Dad had said to me quietly. The remote possibility of family members squabbling over Grampa's things weighed heavily on his head, and he was determined to keep the peace at any cost. He needn't have worried about me. I was interested in only two things. One was the tweed cap Grampa wore year-round on all but the hottest days. I think he'd bought it at Mr. Klemmer's store. Hats seem to reflect and capture something of the people who wear them. I didn't want something that had merely belonged to Grampa Ben; I wanted something that had been a part of him.

The other thing I wanted were any scrapbooks or photo albums that might give me a clue to his past or at least point me in the direction of the young Binyamin Rendsberg and, if I was lucky, to this Benny Leonard guy Mr. Klemmer had mentioned. But I came up empty. Except for a few framed pictures of his late wife (the grandmother I never knew), and his children, and one of his lost family in Nuremberg, there was nothing among Grampa's things that even predated me.

I wandered into the kitchen, hoping I might find a Coke in the fridge. Sure enough there was one bottle left. Grampa hated pop-top cans. He said they were only good for one thing—for wimpy guys to crush and impress their girlfriends. I tried twisting the cap off, but only succeeded in scraping the web between my thumb and forefinger. (Talk about a wimp.) Where to find a bottle opener? No question. Next to the silverware drawer was what Grampa called the Utility Drawer. Translation—the drawer into which you throw anything and everything that doesn't have a place of its own.

Every house has a Utility Drawer, and I'm convinced you can tell a lot about the members of the household by examining what they toss in there. I knew the opener was in there somewhere, but first I had to rummage through pieces of string, rubber bands, half-used tubes of Krazy Glue, old stamps, a peach pit (no kidding), assorted loose change, a couple of wood screws, washers (rubber and metal), batteries of all sizes, a lint-roller, two combs, a fingernail clipper, a half empty box of birthday candles…It would take a day just to catalogue the contents of this drawer. I thought about taking the drawer home and preserving it intact. Lots of people in the world probably had furniture like Grampa's or clothes or tools like his. But nobody had a Utility Drawer like his. Nobody. "Binyamin Rendsberg lived here," I thought as my fingers meandered through the drawer of worthless junk that had suddenly become painfully precious.

I didn't find the bottle opener. But under a deck of Lucky Deal Plasticized Playing Cards I did find a small key attached to a tag that read Chuck's U-Store-It, 325 Kilbourn Rd. Bay #6. Something didn't make sense. There was tons of empty space in the cellar and in the attic. Why would Grampa need to rent space? What did he have that he couldn't (or wouldn't) keep in the house? His (presumed) lost wealth? Some terrible family secret? Amelia Earhart's luggage? The Lost Ark? Only one way to find out.

"Dad, could I take the car?"

"What for?"

"I want to get something to eat."

"Isn't there food in the kitchen?"

"Come on, Dad. Besides I need the practice." I'd gotten my Learner's Permit the week before.

"All right. But be back here in an hour."

Sometimes I'm so clever I scare myself.

I bought some fries and a large Coke (no ice) on the way to Chuck's U-Store-It even though I was too anxious to be hungry. But I'd told Dad I was going to eat something, and I wasn't going to lie to him.

Chuck's consisted of three buildings, each resembling a block of five garages. I drove around until I found an overhead door with a lopsided 6 painted on it and parked. In the glove compartment I found a flashlight which I jammed into the back pocket of my jeans, just in case. As I walked to the door, I couldn't understand why my heart was banging away like it was. I wasn't scared. Or guilty. But as I turned the key in the lock and heard the bolt snap back, I thought about bagging the whole operation.

"Wimp," a voice in my head said.

"You know it," I replied aloud as I lifted the door. Before it cleared eye level, I knew I'd hit the mother lode.

IV

"It's not right," Frau Rendsberg said. "Boxing is for animals, not for civilized human beings and especially not for you. Are you hungry? Have you lived a deprived life? If you were like one of these men who has to fight to feed his family and who has no other skill, that would be one thing. But you, you're lucky. You want for nothing. Someday you will go to a university. You will study and become something that will bring honor to your family. You won't spend your time like a hooligan.

26

"But Mama…," the boy protested weakly, half-looking to his father who was hidden behind the evening paper.

"But nothing," Mama said, shaking a piece of paper in her son's direction. I have to find out from Professor Erdmann. 'Dear Frau. Rendsberg,' he says, 'I hope Binyamin is well. I'm concerned not to have seen him for some time. I hope he has been practicing his scales daily as well as the fingering exercises.' What was I supposed to make of this? You lied to us, Binyamin. We send you to learn the violin, and you spend the money learning to be a street thug. How can we trust you anymore? How?"

"I'm sorry I didn't tell you. But how could I? You would never have let me go to the boxhalle."

"Quite right. And as of this moment you will not set foot in that place again. Am I understood?"

"Please, Mama, don't take this away from me. I used my own money. The money you gave me for the music lessons I put back into your purse."

"So that's…" She stopped for a moment and then decided that her pride in her son's honesty would not dissuade her from her purpose. "No. My son will not hit people for recreation, or, God forbid, be hit."

"Enough. Both of you." Herr Rendsberg folded his paper neatly and set it on the coffee table. "I've heard enough." As his wife and son waited in silence, he carefully packed his pipe with tobacco, lit it, and settled back in his chair with a look of deep concentration. "Binyamin, what you did, deceiving us, was wrong, and you have admitted as much and apologized. That takes character but does not excuse the offense."

Binny lowered his eyes.

"Mama is right. Fighting is a poor way to settle a dispute and an even poorer excuse for a pastime. Our people have always prided themselves on being able to use knowledge, logic, and reason instead of violence. However," he took a long drag on his pipe, "these days it's not a bad idea for a Jew to know how to defend himself. The rabbis always taught me that **pikuach nefesh**, saving a soul, was foremost among the commandments. Against one of these Nazi bullies, a fist might be a surer means of obeying the commandment than a logical argument."

"What are you saying, Otto?"

"I'm not finished." He looked into his youngest son's eyes. "Why do you want to do this, Binyamin? Really."

"Because I'm good, Papa."

"How good?"

"Herr Schiller wants me to start in the Intermediate Class next week. It's supposed to take six months to graduate from the Beginner's level, but it only took me three weeks. My friend Paul is the best fighter in the club, and he says I'm quicker than anyone there. He says…"

Herr Rendsberg raised his hand for silence. "This is my decision, Binyamin. First, you will go to Professor

Erdmann tomorrow, explain your absences, and learn what work must be made up. Second, you will ask Professor Erdmann to reschedule your lesson so as not to conflict with your lessons at the boxhalle."

Frau Rendsberg was aghast. "Otto, you can't be serious."

Her husband raised his hand again, and continued addressing their son.

"If your school grades suffer in the least, boxing is over. If your music suffers, boxing is over. If you are injured, boxing is over. And if you use your fighting skills for anything but self-defense, boxing is over. There will be no argument and no appeal, do you understand?"

"Yes, Papa," said Binny, trying mightily to reign in his joy.

"Now," said Herr Rendsberg, "Give your Mama a kiss and get to your homework."

When the door had shut behind her son, Anna Rendsberg stared at her husband in disbelief.

"How could you do that, Otto? What were you thinking? You want him to come home with a black eye or a broken nose? You want him to be like this Schmeling person, is that it?"

"No, my love," Otto Rendsberg said as his eyes followed the trail of smoke wafting upward from his pipe. "I was thinking he might be the next Benny Leonard."

V

Trophies. Dozens of them. Small ones, big ones, and a couple that had to be over four feet tall, all packed tightly together, like an army of weird gold and silver stalagmites sprouting up from the floor of a fairy-tale cave. The bay was around twenty feet square (it looked bigger from the outside) and the entire floor was covered with them, except for a small area in a rear corner.

That's where the boxes were. Two of them. As I carefully cleared a path through the trophies, thanks to two years of German and a good teacher, I was able to read enough of the inscriptions to be impressed. "First Place," "Champion," "Outstanding Boxer." I knew he'd been good, but this was incredible. Did Dad know about all this? I passed the two four-footers. Each consisted of a hefty square wooden base, a shiny golden bowl with ornate handles resting on a gold pedestal, and a ten-inch figure of a boxer perched on top. Fine scrollwork covered them from top to bottom. They were the most beautiful trophies I'd ever seen (not that I'd seen all that many). One bowl was inscribed "1934" and the other "1935." On the bases the plates read "B. Rendsberg—Champione du Deutschland. 60 Kg."

"Why, Grampa? Why'd you hide this?" For the first time, I felt like an intruder. This was his secret place, a shrine to a past he'd closed the book on, and I had no right to be here. If Dad didn't know about Bay #6, I'd have to tell him and hope that he wouldn't tell anyone else.

When I reached the rear of the bay, I held the flashlight between my teeth, and opened the first box. It was full of medals. Completely full. Some were loose, some were attached to ribbons, some rested in velvet lined boxes. All were thrown together like so much cast off junk. I couldn't guess at how many there were. A stray thought occurred to me. If Grampa hadn't cared about any of this stuff, why did he bother to keep it? I had come here for answers and was succeeding only in stirring up more questions.

I opened the second box and knew my search was over.

Scrapbooks. Six of them, one for each year from 1931 through 1936, bulging with clippings, old fight programs, newspaper headlines, and ancient photographs. All but the last one. The volume labeled 1936 seemed empty. I had to remind myself to breathe. I lifted one of the volumes from the box and opened it as carefully and tenderly as a father holding his infant son for the first time. I didn't get past the first picture. 1931. There he was, young and slim and full of promise, so magnificent in his old-fashioned boxing togs, staring unsmiling at the camera, arms folded, chin angled slightly up. Years away from meet-

31

ing Grandma, two decades away from knowing his son, two generations away from knowing me. Even in the darkness of Chuck's U-Store-It, the photo had become faded and washed out, but it didn't matter.

"Hi, Grampa," I said to the picture. "You don't know me yet, but you will."

I cried more then than I had at his funeral.

VI

December, 1931. After less than a year of training, Binyamin Rendsberg took his place as the lightweight on the Nuremberg Boxhalle's competition squad. Herr Schiller, sensing something unique about the boy, was determined to see that his protege's talent was fully realized. Many a promising fighter had climbed high on the mountain only to slide off because of an inflated ego, lack of discipline, or faltering commitment. Herr Schiller promised himself this would not happen with his star lightweight.

It was Herr Schiller who first told Binyamin Rendsberg about Benny Leonard.

"He's the greatest lightweight who ever lived," he told Binny after a workout. "He took the title from Freddie Welsh in 1917 and retired with it in 1925. And he didn't just sit on it. The first year alone he defended it every month. Not once or twice a year like most champs.

There were a lot of good lightweights then, a lot of them, and the belt seemed to change hands every couple of years or so until Leonard won it. Seven and a half years he held it. Unbelievable. And," Herr Schiller leaned forward, "it was the first time many had spoken the name of a Jew with respect."

Binny shifted his feet uneasily. Since he had joined the team his trainer had never made any reference to his religion, and though what was said was positive, Binny still felt a twinge of self-consciousness. Herr Schiller had often said that students in his boxhalle were to behave properly inside and outside the ring, and that meant liking or disliking a person based on what he did, not what he was. "We are a team," he was fond of saying. "Though you fight as individuals, your efforts must be for the common good. You are all Germans. You are all athletes. Grasp for greatness together. A single twig may be easily broken. But bind many twigs together, and they have strength." No one in the boxhalle had ever made a comment about Binny's religion, not to his face anyway, so when Herr Schiller did so, Binny couldn't help feeling a little uncomfortable.

"Leonard has had something like 200 fights and I think he's lost four. Some bouts he won with power, some he won with finesse. He could do anything. His first two fights he got flattened. But that's the mark of a champion, Binny. Coming back. Anyone can run up a string, ten, fifteen wins in a row. I've seen it a thousand times. Then the guy loses once, gets beaten really badly, and he shrivels up like a leaf in autumn and blows away. Suddenly his ego can't handle the fact that he's not invincible anymore, and he becomes afraid. But to lose and then to climb back on the horse…few can do it. Leonard did. His longest streak was 150 straight fights without a loss. After the loss, he went on to win the title and to become the greatest lightweight that God ever put on the earth."

Herr Schiller sighed. "He thinks he can go on forever."

"I thought you said he retired."

"He did. The newspapers say it was because his mother asked him to quit because she was afraid he'd get hurt. Nice story. Only partially true. The fact is, he had made a fortune and was at the peak of his power when he quit. He'd beaten everyone and had no more worlds to conquer. At that moment he knew he had climbed as high as he could, and could do nothing more except slide down, so he wisely hung his gloves on a nail and went home. For a while, life was good. But then he lost all his money when the American stock market crashed in 1929, and last year he had to start fighting again. He hadn't done any exercise in five years. He'd put on pounds that he couldn't get rid of, so he's had to move up to welterweight. Thus far he's done all right, seven or eight wins, but he hasn't fought any real contenders yet. So now the Great Benny Leonard is fighting to eat, just like any ordinary pug. Eventually, within a *year I believe, he'll have to fight a quality opponent, and when that happens he will lose. Badly, I'm afraid.*

"The body is a liar, Binny. As you get older you can't tell when your speed and strength and reflexes begin to desert you. I have a friend who lost a leg to a grenade in the Great War. For months afterward he said he could still feel the leg itching and tingling, even though it wasn't there anymore. I'm sure Benny Leonard feels the same way, wondering why he's getting hit with punches he used to slip without thinking, why the punches that used to lay his opponents out flat now only makes them shake their heads. But oh, how great he was."

Herr Schiller smiled and shook his head sadly. He looked across his desk and saw a strange look in Binny's eyes.

"You want to know if you can be that good, don't you? As good as Benny Leonard."

Binny said nothing, but Herr Schiller had read his protege well.

"There are good fighters and great fighters, Binyamin. And then there are those who transcend greatness, those whose presence change the sport forever. They show us how pure boxing can be, how like life itself. They show us a kernel of beauty within the brutality. Nothing is the same after them. Other fighters try to copy them, and people on the street speak their names in awe. They see further than the rest of us, because they have risen above us. They pass into myth, these few. Why? Because in a

*world where it seems the goal is to be average, they
approach perfection, and that brings them closer to
God. For those of us who worship boxing, they push
ahead the boundaries of human achievement to realms
undreamed of, and leave us wondering what the next
Benny Leonard will reveal." Herr Schiller looked Binny
in the eye. "And there <u>will</u> be another. Someday. That's
all I can say."*

VII

I left the scrapbooks in the storage bay for later
retrieval, pocketed the pilfered key, and drove back to
Grampa's house faster than anyone (much less someone with only a learner's permit) should drive. Dad,
Mom, my aunts and cousins had pretty much gone
through everything and decided who was going to
take what, what was going to charity, and which real
estate agency would handle the disposition of the
house. Everything seemed the picture of harmony,
and I had no intention of possibly upsetting the cart.

Later, when we were back home, alone, Dad said, "I
have something for you," and he handed me
Grampa's cap.

"I have something for you, too," I said fishing the
key out of my jeans and handing it to him. "Can I
take you for a drive? Just you? I need practice."

He turned the key over in his hand once or twice and handed it back, eyeing me with a quizzical expression. Obviously, he didn't know about the trophy trove.

"Sure," he said suspiciously, tossing me the car keys. "Let's go for a ride."

It was late dusk when we pulled up to bay #6. Dad took the flashlight, and I all but vaulted from the car, I was so anxious for him to see what I'd found.

"Do you know anything about this place?" I asked him.

He shook his head. "What am I supposed to know?"

"Brace yourself," I said as I raised the door and watched as his jaw sagged.

"My God, what in the name of…? How did you…"

"I found the key in a drawer in the kitchen and let curiosity do the rest."

"I never knew. I can't believe I never knew."

"The best is yet to come," I said. "Wait here." I sidled my way through the trophies as I had earlier in the afternoon, and with Dad in the doorway holding the flashlight as high as he could, I brought out the box that would soon help me unlock the door to my grandfather's past. "Take a look at this."

To say that Dad was stunned would be to state the obvious. He was in shock.

"There's one for each year from 1931 through 1936," I told him, but I doubt he heard me. He was lost among the images of his father, images his father had successfully kept from the family for decades for reasons only he knew. "I haven't looked through them all very carefully yet. I know the first four are packed. 1935 is maybe half-full and 1936 is empty."

A thought occurred to me. Did Mr. Klemmer know about Bay #6? Could he shed some light on all this? Why didn't I think of him earlier? All roads seemed to be leading back to Grampa's best friend.

"I need a favor, Dad."

"Sure, son," Dad said, replacing the book and pulling a Kleenex from his pocket.

"I'd like to go through these books before we tell anyone else about them. I'll only need a few days, maybe a week. I'm trying to find out some stuff about Grampa, and it may be here."

"What are you looking for?"

"His life before he came to Boston."

"Take whatever time you need. I wish I could help you, but I don't know anything. Pop never liked to talk about his life in the old country."

"That's okay. But all this is our secret for the time being, right?"

"Absolutely." And with that he reached over the box and hugged me. Tight. I always knew that Dad loved me, but he never said so. It wasn't his style. I think that hug was as close as he ever came.

VII

"*I know little of sports and nothing about boxing,*" Herr Rendsberg said to his son. "*And yet even I know of Benny Leonard. More than that, I admire him. What conclusions can you draw?*"

"*That he was very famous?*" Binny answered tenuously.

"*Indeed. What else?*"

"*He was great.*"

"*Certainly, but you miss the point. What would cause an athlete, even an exceptional one like Benny Leonard, to be talked about and respected by people who have no interest whatsoever in his sport?*"

Binny thought hard, but came up empty. "*I don't know, Papa.*"

"*Think.*"

"*I am thinking.*" Binny scratched his head. "*If he was famous outside boxing, then maybe he was also great at something outside boxing.*"

"*That's what I was after. I would expect Herr Schiller to praise Leonard's athletic excellence. I, however, am much more impressed with Mr. Leonard's greatness as a human being and as a Jew.*"

"*What did he do?*"

"*He knocked down barriers.*"

"*That's what Herr Schiller told me.*"

"*Not boxing barriers, Binny. Barriers that said Jews are only good at certain things—commerce, medicine,*

law. Barriers that said Jews won't fight if attacked. Barriers that have kept our people subservient for centuries. These are not only limitations that others have imposed on us. They are chains with which we have shackled ourselves. I remember a story, I think by Kipling, I'm not sure. A baby elephant was captured and tethered to a stake with a heavy chain. He pulled and pulled but could not break free. As he grew, his handlers replaced the chain with a rope which the elephant could have snapped with a single tug of its leg. But the animal never tried to break free because it believed it couldn't."

"And what has Benny Leonard to do with all that?"

"He showed us we could break free. Slavery is not only physical, it's mental. Why did the Jews wander in the desert for forty years?"

"Because they worshipped the golden calf."

"On the surface, yes. But in fact they were not intellectually ready to be self-sufficient. Their bodies were free but their minds were still in Egypt. That's why they kept whining to go back. Benny Leonard showed the world that there is no such thing as a typical Jew. And he showed us that there is no field at which we cannot excel."

"If that weren't enough, for the first time, we had a hero who didn't have his nose in a book. A gentle man in a brutal profession who took pride in being a Jew when most Jews tried to hide who they were. He defeated stereotypes, Binny, not just other boxers. And when he won, we won."

VIII

Even with my two years of German I knew I'd never be able to translate all the stuff Grampa had accumulated in his scrapbooks. So I told Mr. Dreier, my German teacher, about my find, hoping to get some help. He was great. I wanted to bring one or two books to his house, but Mr. Dreier said to bring everything. After leafing through some of the material and seeing that many of the clippings were extremely brittle, he said we really ought to put everything onto a computer before the paper became powder.

Every day for a week he dictated and I typed. Or to be more accurate, he dictated, I typed, and he waited for me to finish. I'd never been on an odyssey before, but I think this exercise qualified as one.

The material in the 1931 volume was pretty generic. Anytime the Nuremberg Boxhalle, its team, or any of its members found their way into newsprint, the article found its way into this album. The photos were funny and wonderful. Shots of Grampa, the baby of the family, wearing a three-piece suit and boxing gloves, standing between his two older (and considerably larger brothers). Grampa, in the same outfit, standing beside his father. No photo with his mother, however. There were badly lit pictures taken at the gym where he trained, and at the end of the book, a formal portrait taken in front of a floral backdrop with Grampa in black tights and tank top, satin sash and shorts, his skinny arms folded across his chest, his face devoid of emotion.

Threaded through the albums were some pretty noticeable trends. In 1931 the team had showed promise, anchored by Paul Klemmer, who almost never lost. In fact, he almost never won by a decision. It was knockout after knockout.

Grampa had done well, but he wasn't a star yet. His most interesting victory that year was in a match against a team from Bremen.

*(you think I'm like that dumb **shlub** from Bremen)*

Amateur bouts are three rounds long and for two rounds Grampa was apparently whipping his opponent pretty handily. But in the last round a looping left hook sent him reeling into a corner and onto the canvas. He got to his feet and amazingly beckoned to the other fighter to move in on him. The other guy didn't know what to make of the gesture. Was it a trap? A bluff? In the few seconds the guy took to ponder his dilemma, Grampa was apparently able to shake the cobwebs out of his head. He lasted the round and won the fight. Afterward, when a reporter asked him about his unconventional tactics, Grampa told him he didn't remember the knockdown or the way he'd psyched his opponent. He'd acted on instinct. That kind of presence of mind was not lost on the reporters covering the match. That year his record had been 16-5.

In the 1932 book, most of the pictures were of Grampa and Mr. Klemmer together. By the end of the year they were being called Nuremberg's one-two punch. Much was made of their talent inside the ring and their friendship outside of it. Also in this particular volume was an article about Benny Leonard, the man Mr. Klemmer had told me to research. Leonard had been a lightweight champion, had come out of retirement, and at age 36, had been matched against the number one welterweight contender, Jimmy McLarnin. According to the article, Leonard had won the first three or four rounds before McLarnin caught up with him in the sixth and had knocked Benny to his knees where he'd been counted out. After the fight he announced he was retiring for good.

That year, Grampa lost only two of thirty bouts. The Nuremberg coach said he liked to keep his boys active.

In 1933 Grampa had his first undefeated year, winning twenty-eight straight, and the Nuremberg one-two punch took their team to the Intermediate Division Championship. In the National Tournament the team finished fifth out of over twenty teams. Teams from Berlin, Munich, and Hamburg had finished ahead of Nuremberg, but Nuremberg caught the fancy of the press. They characterized the squad from the Nuremberg Boxhalle as David going after the Goliaths of German boxing. "With Rendsberg and

Klemmer as the team's foundation," said a Berlin sportswriter, "it's only a matter of time until Clement Schiller's charges start knocking off some of the bigger boys on the block."

He was right.

In 1934, Nuremberg Boxhalle took the national title from Berlin, and Grampa and Mr. Klemmer were crowned champions. A picture showed a slightly disheveled Grampa after his championship bout with one arm being held aloft by the referee and the other by Mr. Klemmer, who could not have looked happier. Grampa went undefeated again that year, and the articles said that barring unforeseen circumstances, he and Mr. Klemmer were shoo-ins for the Olympic team and probably for Gold Medals.

In the summer of 1935 Grampa and Mr. Klemmer retained their titles, but the Nuremberg team came in second to Berlin who claimed three individual champions. The articles again praised the Nuremberg duo's prowess (Grampa had been named Outstanding Boxer of the tournament), and predicted success in the Olympic Trials the following spring and in the Games the following summer.

The last half of the album was empty.

I'd thought the 1936 book was completely empty, but flipping through the pages I found something I'd missed—a single page on which a two-inch summary of the Olympic Trials was pasted. Names and weight classes only. Grampa wasn't on the list. Neither was Mr. Klemmer.

As Mr. Dreier and I wound up our efforts, instead of the sense of satisfaction I thought I'd be feeling, I was frustrated. I felt like I'd opened a box full of jigsaw puzzle pieces, only to find they'd come from three different puzzles, none of them complete. Mr. Klemmer was my only hope, but I was almost reluctant to see him. If he couldn't fill in the spaces, I'd have to live with the unsolved riddle of my grandfather for the rest of my life. Each generation of our family to come would know less and less of Binyamin Rendsberg, until at some point somewhere in the future, the few remaining fragments of his life that were still lodged in someone's memory would quietly blow away for lack of something to hold them together.

I gave myself a day to find out what I could about Benny Leonard. After that, it would be up to Paul Klemmer to seal the final chapter in the life of his best friend.

IX

Binny walked through the front door whistling. His parents were waiting for him. He'd never seen them looking so grim.

"What's the matter? What's happened?"

"We need to talk with you, Son," his father said. "Sit down, please."

"Is someone sick? Has someone…"

"No everyone is fine. As fine as we can be, considering the circumstances."

Frau Rendsberg who hadn't said a word, left the room, crying softly into her handkerchief.

"Binny, today the Nazis held a meeting here in Nuremberg. They've put out a new list of restrictions for us. We can no longer hold jobs in the government. We cannot vote. We can't serve in the army. Jews may no longer marry non-Jews or employ German women as servants. To put it bluntly—we are no longer citizens of our own country. It is only a matter of time until they isolate us completely from the rest of the population."

Binny sat in silence. His brothers had been saying for some time that the family should leave and go to France or England or America until Germany regained its senses. Papa had dismissed this kind of talk as paranoia, but Binny could tell his father was having a change of mind.

"Don't worry, Papa. We'll manage."

"You're right, we'll get by. But I'm concerned about you."

"Why? I'll get by, too." He managed a smile.

"You don't understand, Binny. They want us to be separate in every walk of life." Herr Rendsberg turned away from his son. He did not want to see the boy's face. "Within a few days or weeks, I expect…" The words stuck in his throat. "I expect you will not be allowed to enter the boxhalle or train with the other boys or participate in competitions."

Binny's face turned the color of wax.

"But I'm the champion of Germany. Twice."

"You're a Jew."

"A German Jew."

"A Jew. That's all they see."

"No. Herr Schiller won't just lock me out."

"He will not have a choice. He will do as they say, or they will close the boxhalle. Or burn it."

Binny had never spoken in anger to his father, but there was no stemming the rage that poured from him.

"Haven't I brought honor to this city and to my team?"

"Yes, great honor."

"And yet you think so little of them that you would say such things. They are my friends. They will not stand by and do nothing. They will fight for me as I have fought for them. We are all Germans."

"I hope you're right," said Herr Rendsberg as his son ran to his room and slammed the door.

X

"Hello."

"Hello, Mr. Klemmer?"

"Yes."

"Hi, it's…"

"You think I don't know who it is? You think my brain is getting soft?" I could hear a smile in his voice. "I expected to hear from you sooner."

"I was going to call you, but some things came up."

"And?"

"And I think it's time we talked."

"You did what I told you?"

"I did some reading about Benny Leonard, yes."

"Okay. Come tomorrow noon. We'll have lunch. You like tuna?"

"Sure, but you don't have to…"

"It's better to discuss serious things over food. Be on time."

"Should I bring anything?"

There was a second or two of dead air on the line.

"You got a cassette recorder?" he asked.

"Uh huh."

"Bring it. What I'm going to tell you, I will say once and once only. I will repeat nothing. So unless you know shorthand, come prepared."

"This sounds awfully mysterious," I said with a chuckle.

"Noon," he said curtly as he cut us off.

XI

The boxhalle was noisy but not as noisy as it should have been. It was a bad sign, because this was one place where nothing ever changed. Routine ruled. Unless something was wrong.

Binny went to his locker. The strip of adhesive tape with his name on it that had been affixed to the locker door four years earlier was gone.

Paul was sitting on the far end of the bench slowly wrapping his hands. Too slowly.

Binny dialed the lock's combination and unlatched the door. He needn't have bothered. The reverberation inside the locker told him it was empty. He looked at his friend, his best friend, who couldn't meet his eyes. Words would have been superfluous.

Herr Schiller sat with his elbows on his desktop, his face in his hands. A large duffel bag containing Binny's gear rested against the wall.

"All my life I dreamed of training a fighter like you. All my life." Unlike Paul, Herr Schiller was able to meet his star pupil's eyes. Later Binny would be grateful for that. "I had to choose between losing you or losing the club."

"Did they tell you that?"

"They didn't have to. It was coming."

"But they didn't actually say it."

"I know how they work, these scum. They…"

"You gave up without a word, didn't you?" Binny spoke calmly, but there was acid in his voice. "You threw in the towel. You train us to fight, and you surrender with a whimper."

"I am coach of this boxhalle," Herr Schiller roared leaping to his feet. His voice cracked and his eyes were bloodshot. The two looked at each other, the student and the teacher, one with anger, the other with anguish. Herr Schiller sank back into his seat, and Binny slowly slung the duffel over his shoulder.

"Show them, Binny. Show them that you're made out of better stuff than the rest of us. Be a champion."

"I already am a champion, or have you forgotten?"

"Olympic champion."

"How? They won't let…"

"They have to let you participate in the trials. The International Olympic Committee rules forbid discrimination, and the Nazis won't do anything to jeopardize the games. You'll have to train on your own, but if anyone can do it, it's you. Show them, Binny. The trials are in six months. Show them."

Binny left the office. He had grown in many ways since first entering this place with his violin case four years earlier. But without looking left or right, he walked out. Some of the faces in the gym were long, but they all watched him go, and none said a word.

Herr Schiller closed the door to his office, locked it, turned out the lights, and drove his fist into the wall, shattering most of the bones in his hand.

"My son," he whispered as he sagged to the floor.

XII

"More soda?"

"No thanks, I'm full."

"Thank you for bringing these. All my pictures were left behind in Germany. I never knew Binny had these."

Mr. Klemmer had leafed through the albums, his gnarled fingers passing loving over the images of his youth and the youth of his friend. His demeanor was one of fond reminiscence until he came to the 1935 volume. Quite perceptibly his face darkened, and it seemed to require some effort for him to wade through the final entries. The single clipping in the 1936 album, the listing of the winners of the 1936 Olympic Trials, held his attention for some time, despite its small size.

"I wasn't surprised that Grampa's name wasn't there," I said. "But I thought I'd see yours."

"No. It was not to be."

"You said the Nazis didn't keep him off the team."

"That's correct."

"Did he try out?"

"Yes."

"He took part in the trials?"

"Yes."

I looked at the clipping, at the name of the light-weight winner. "Did this guy beat Grampa?"

"No."

"Someone else beat him, then."

"No."

"Wait a second, Mr. Klemmer. You're saying that Grampa entered the trials, that no one beat him, but that he still didn't make the team? That doesn't make sense."

"Sometimes life plays tricks. Bitter tricks. If we're smart we learn from them, but sometimes we get smart too late. I must tell you that in the months between when Binny left the boxhalle and the Olympic trials I hardly spoke to him. Maybe once or twice. I wanted to see more of him. Help him work out. At least try to pick up his spirits. But I didn't. He was my friend, but I didn't know what to say. And...," he paused. I didn't know whether he was searching for the right words, or deciding whether or not to let the words he had come out. "And I think I was self-ishly grateful that I could still train. Whatever, I was a coward. We all were. But especially me."

The silence was long and awkward.

"Would you mind if I started the tape recorder?"

"Go ahead."

I put a cassette into the machine, set the mike in the middle of the table, and pressed Record.

XIII

The attic became his boxhalle. He had no heavy bag on which to work his punches, but he filled his duffel with sawdust and hung it from the rafters. It sufficed. The long mirror from his mother's closet went upstairs, too, so he could shadowbox his reflection and check his form. He could still run, stretch, and do his calisthenics. And despite the family's dwindling resources, Frau Rendsberg saw to it that Binny's diet wasn't compromised.

The only thing lacking was sparring. And the atmosphere. There was no way Binny could replace Herr Schiller's discipline and regimentation. And he desperately missed the sounds and smells of the boxhalle. But he was a champion. A champion. There was no word in the language like it. No other word conveyed the same sense of sacrifice and achievement and triumph. He'd been cut adrift, but the word kept his head above water.

Champion. Champion he had been, champion he was, and champion he would be again.

A few weeks before the trials, Binny stepped on the bathroom scale and gasped as the dial went to 63 kilos, well past the lightweight limit of 60. How could it be possible? He hadn't stepped on the scale for a while because his weight had never varied more than half a kilo. He was training harder than ever and eating right. He looked in the mirror. He was still lean and hard with no trace of fat. The scale had to be defective.

Unless…

He ran to his closet and put on his best suit jacket. The sleeves stopped well above his wrists. He had grown.

He had two courses of action. He could try to drop the weight by cutting back his carbohydrate intake. But his body would have less fuel to burn and he'd tire earlier and easier. Or he could add another two or three kilos and fight as a welterweight. Carrying additional weight would make his punches stronger but would slow his legs. The choice was obvious. He had to move up.

XIV

Mr. Klemmer continued, "About five or six weeks before the trials, Herr Schiller came to me and said he was making some changes. The team title at the Olympic Trials was very prized because like the Games themselves, the trials were held only once every four years. It wasn't uncommon for a coach to shuffle his roster to get the greatest use of all his boxers. And unlike most of the other boys, my weight could go up or down five or eight pounds, and it never bothered me. I was still strong. So he moved me around a lot, mostly up. I enjoyed fighting as a light-heavyweight. It's gratifying to beat someone who's bigger than you are.

At middleweight, besides me, we had a fellow named Gunther Scharbach. A very good fighter, but I was better. Herr Schiller knew that not only could I probably beat any other middleweight in the world, Gunther could also do very well.

"Paul," I remember him saying. "I'm going to enter Gunther at middleweight. I want you to go…"

I finished his sentence. "To light-heavy?"

"No," he said. "I want you to drop a class to 67 kilos."

Welterweight.

XV

At the Olympic Trials the fighters in each weight class were first seeded according to their records and past performances, and then separated into two pools, the number one seed being placed in one pool and the number two seed in the other. The winners of each pool (the top two seeds, most likely) would meet in the finals. In the welterweight division, the Organizing Committee had seeded Paul Klemmer number one, and Binyamin

Rendsberg number two, based on Paul's superior strength and knockout percentage.

Also, Rendsberg had not competed in six months.

The two reached the finals without incident. Binny knocked out his first opponent and decisioned the next two to reach the final. Paul scored three easy knockouts, two in the first round.

They would meet to decide who would represent Germany in the Olympic Games.

XVI

"You two fought each other?"

Mr. Klemmer nodded grimly.

A stray thought registered.

"Wait a second," I said grabbing the 1936 album and opening it to the lone clipping. Something I had barely noticed before hit me between the eyes.

WELTERWEIGHT (67) kilos—NO WINNER. DISQUALIFICATION.

I looked blankly at Mr. Klemmer.

"What happened?"

He cast a glance at the tape recorder and began unloading the baggage he'd been carrying for more than half a century.

XVII

The referee motioned them to the center of the ring. Paul was accompanied by Werner Plockmann, one of Herr Schiller's assistant trainers, and Binny was seconded by his father. Herr Rendsberg, of course, had little to do. Between rounds he would hold the spit bucket, rinse the mouthguard, wipe his son's face, and smear a little grease on the boy's cheekbones and around the eyes. The grease cut down on friction from punches, and kept the skin from splitting.

"I want a clean fight," said the referee to the fighters and their seconds. "You know the rules. No blows below the belt or shots to the kidneys. Watch the elbows and head butts, especially in the clinches. In the event of a knockdown, the fighter standing must go to the nearest neutral corner before I begin the count. Is all that understood?"

Nods all around.

"Good. You two are the cream of this tournament. Let's see a bout worthy of your talents. Good luck. Shake hands, come out fighting, and may the better man win."

Binny and Paul touched gloves and turned their backs on each other without a word or a look.

In the corner, Herr Rendsberg asked his son, "Do you know what Paul is being told by his second?"

"To win."

"Yes. For nine minutes you must put your friendship aside."

"What friendship?"

The bell rang.

Paul roared out of his corner like a locomotive, shoulders hunched forward, his left hand chest high, his right cocked under his chin. Binny was up on his toes, moving laterally, side to side, flicking his left jab out like a snake's tongue. The jab isn't a power punch. It doesn't hurt. But it throws the other man's timing off and briefly obstructs his vision. And it opens cuts. The pattern for the first round was set early with Binny jabbing and occasionally following up with a right, and Paul stalking, throwing few punches, and forcing Binny to keep moving. Near the end of the round, Paul dug a left hook into Binny's ribs, pulling Binny's hands down, and then threw the hook over the top. Binny pulled back, but he still caught enough of the punch to know he'd be on the deck if the punch had landed full. When Paul moved in, Binny grabbed him in a clinch. "Is that as hard as you can hit?" he hissed in Paul's ear.

Paul twisted with a grunt and angrily threw Binny into the ropes. The referee jumped between them and yelled at Paul "This is not a wrestling match. Pull that kind of thing again, and it'll cost you a point, understand?"

Paul nodded as the bell rang.

In the corner, Werner Plockmann was furious.

"I can't believe you fell for that. He's playing you for a chump. Now the ref's going to be watching you like a hawk."

"I'm sorry, I lost my head."

"Well screw it back on. Work his body, understand? Work the body, and the head will fall. Quit being a headhunter. Punch his guts out. I don't want him to be able to eat anything but soup for a week, got it?"

Paul nodded as his handler reinserted the mouth-piece.

"Now go out there and knock that little Jew on his ass."

The second round began as a replay of the first, Binny sticking the jab and moving, Paul trying to cut the ring off and land the big punch. But mid-way through the round, Binny began loading up and throwing heavier punches. "Heavier punches get more points from the judges," he told himself, thinking that if the bout were close, there was no way the judges would award him the decision. He had to win convincingly, if not by a knock-out. But the truth was that he was getting tired. The lack of sparring and the added weight were sapping his legs. So in the middle of the round, he made the decision that would cost him the fight. He came down off his toes and began slugging.

Paul couldn't believe it. It had to be a trick. Binny would never try to trade punches with him. Punching power comes from standing with the front foot flat, but by standing flat-footed, Binny was sacrificing his great-est asset—his mobility. His punches were sharp and strong. But Paul was used to taking shots from mid-dleweights, so even with the added power, Binny's punches hardly bothered Paul at all. They were confusing, but they took no physical toll. And nothing demoralizes a fighter more than when an opponent takes his best punch, shakes it off, and keeps coming. So when Binny teed off on Paul's head with a hook that would have laid out any other welterweight in the world, and Paul blinked once and came boring in again, Binny knew he was in trouble.

He got back up onto his toes and tried to dance again, but his speed had deserted him, and his calves felt like they were on fire. Paul, with the instinct of a predator, cut the ring off and trapped his opponent along the ropes. All Binny could do was cover up and try to survive the round.

It wasn't to be.

Two vicious body blows emptied Binny's lungs, and a textbook-perfect right cross dropped him to the canvas. Face first.

There are few absolutes in boxing, but one of them says when a man goes down face first, he doesn't get up. Herr Plockmann leaped with jubilation, arms extended overhead, Herr Rendsberg, seeing his son lying motionless, vomited into the spit bucket, and the referee moved in yelling "Neutral corner, Klemmer. Move!"

But Paul didn't budge.

"Get going." The referee took Paul's arm and tried to push him toward the corner. But Paul jerked his arm free and stood his ground.

"I'm not going to start the count until you get out of here!" the referee screamed.

Werner Plockmann scrambled up onto the ring apron.

"What the hell's the matter with you? Get to the corner! Now!"

Paul turned to Werner Plockmann, and with a sneer of disgust, spat his mouthpiece at his handler, hitting him in the forehead.

"You want to move me, get a gun, you little pig."

The referee looked helplessly toward the judges. No one knew what to do. Finally, the head of the German Olympic Boxing Federation ran to the timekeeper's table and repeatedly rang the bell. He, the judges, and the referee conferred for less than a minute.

Paul remained motionless, glowering defiantly at the referee and the judges. Herr Rendsberg had climbed through the ropes and was passing a small bottle of ammonia under his son's nose. Binny began to stir, blinking his eyes and trying to clear the fog from his brain.

The crowd noise which had been deafening had turned to an eerie near-silence. Somewhere in the crowd, a lone individual began applauding slowly. It was Herr Schiller. He rose to his feet, continuing to applaud, slamming his good hand against his cast with greater and greater force. Spectators around him began to hoot and pelt him with crumpled programs and half-eaten food.

Two days later he would be relieved of his position at the Nuremberg Boxhalle and sent to a small public school in the remote Black Forest region where, for the remainder of his life, he would teach exercise to elementary school children and act as the school's janitor.

A voice came over the loudspeakers.

"Ladies and gentlemen, the judges have ruled unanimously that this bout has ended in a double disqualification."

Paul peeled off his gloves, flung them into the crowd, and left the ring.

XVIII

Mr. Klemmer leaned back in his chair. The only sounds in his kitchen were the muffled whir of the tape recorder and the hum of his electric wall clock. I cast about in my head for something to say, something that would help me to understand what I'd just learned.

I was grateful when he broke the silence.

"Don't make me out to be more than I am."

"But you gave up…"

"I gave up what? A medal that would end up in the bottom of a drawer under my shirts?"

"No, I was thinking you gave up the glory of being an Olympic champion."

64

His head moved in an almost imperceptible nod.

"Yes," he said softly. "But at what price?" As he spoke he pushed the crumbs around on his plate with his thumb, first to one side then to another, sometimes forming them into little piles and sometimes into shapeless designs. "Binny never was the same. He'd never been hurt before. And he'd never been afraid. But that fight taught him fear. And he knew that the fear would keep him an amateur forever. A great one, certainly. But he'd never make it as a professional. He could never be Benny Leonard."

Mr. Klemmer looked at me. "I did it to him, you know. I did the worst thing one human being can do to another, outside of taking his life. I destroyed his dream. He never fought again. Many times he told me he never missed the old days, his glory days, but I didn't believe him. And now with what you've found, the pictures and the trophies, I know I was right." He smiled. "The applause of the crowd never leaves your ears. Never."

More than anything I wished I could say something comforting to Mr. Klemmer, come up with some combination of words that would somehow lighten the load he'd been carrying around for so long. Wisely, for a change, I kept my mouth shut. Better to say nothing than the wrong thing.

Mr. Klemmer abruptly sat bolt upright and smacked both palms on his knees.

"Anyway, a year later, 1937, his parents shipped him off to America to a cousin in Boston, supposedly to pave the way for the whole family to come over. They weren't wealthy, the Rendsbergs. But the Nazis assumed all Jews were rich, and Binny's father knew the authorities would never let the entire family out of the country, fearing they'd take their fortune with them. So he figured the best course of action was to send the youngest son alone. A lot of strings were pulled and a lot of officials bribed to get Binny out, but he made it."

"You said Grampa was sent here *supposedly* to pave the way. What do you mean 'supposedly'?"

"What I mean is the whole thing was a ploy. Herr Rendsberg knew that his family was never going to leave Germany alive. And if he couldn't save the whole family he'd save one son, if only to keep the Rendsberg name alive. So he convinced Binny that the cousin in America would help get things in order. A week after the boat took Binny to America, the Nazis rounded up all the Jews in the city and took them away. I don't know where the Rendsbergs ended up or what happened to them, but I never saw them again."

"How do you know all this?"

"A couple of days after Binny had gone, I visited his parents to see if they'd had any word from him. They hadn't. It was then that Herr Rendsberg handed me an envelope containing a letter meant for his son in the event that ill fortune should befall the family. He was a very astute man. He knew the noose was tightening around them. When I promised to deliver the letter personally, he told me what I've just told you."

"Did you ever tell Grampa?"

"Of course not. How could I tell him such a thing. Whatever was in the envelope would be enough. Besides he was such a realist, he figured it out. And when he did and the war was over and the horrors of the camps became known, he stopped going to the synagogue. Some days he'd say that God was to blame, and other days he'd say that God didn't exist at all. Eventually he came to believe that there was still a God in the world after all, but not the God he'd prayed to in his youth. That's why he stopped going to any synagogue. He believed in God, but didn't know who God was anymore."

"I wish we'd found the letter among Grampa's things. I wonder what was in it."

"I have no idea. Binny was greatly loved by his family. I assume the letter reaffirmed that. I kept it with me all during the war years as I moved around from place to place, trying to keep some distance between myself and the army recruiters who were always on my tail. And when the war was over, I came out of hiding and booked passage on the first boat to America."

He picked up his cup and took a swallow of very cold coffee.

"Bleh," he exclaimed. "Let me put the pot on. I'll make us some tea." As he went to the stove I shut off the tape recorder.

"Got more than you bargained for, didn't you?" he said as he filled his small pot from the kitchen faucet.

"Yes." I was drained. "But I'm really grateful."

"Me, too. Your tape machine is off so I assume you have no more questions?"

"No, I think we've covered everything."

"Good. The water will boil in a couple of minutes." He opened the cabinet over the stove and scanned the contents. "I've got herbal, regular, decaffeinated…"

"I think I'd better be going."

"Okay. You'll take a raincheck?"

"You bet."

As we walked to the door I remembered something.

"You wouldn't happen to know what became of his money, would you? Supposedly he sold the stores for a pretty sizable profit, but he never seemed to spend much on himself. Any ideas?"

"A man should never concern himself with another man's wallet. His business was his, and my business was mine, and that's the way we kept it. Maybe that's why we stayed friends for so long."

"You two were really lucky to have each other."

He shrugged.

"And all those years you never mentioned any of this to anyone?"

"No. And I never will again."

"But why?"

"Because it was Binny's life and his responsibility to tell, not mine. But now that he's gone, I'll stick my nose in his business this once because it's important that you and your family come to know the truth. All of it."

"Thanks, Mr. Klemmer," I said shaking his hand. "I wish I could do something to pay you back."

"You want to do something for me? Mow my grass next week."

I grinned for the first time in a long while.

"Deal."

XIX

In 1932, immediately after losing the fight to Jimmy McLarnin, Benny Leonard announced his retirement, and never fought again. In 209 fights, he had lost only 6 times. Many boxing authorities name him as pound for pound the greatest boxer who ever lived.

On April 18, 1947, while refereeing his sixth bout of the evening at the St. Nicholas Arena in New York, he suffered a heart attack and died. On many occasions he had been quoted as saying that when his time came, he wanted to die in the ring.

He got his wish.

He was 51 years old.

XX

In Israel, near Tel Aviv there is a large athletic complex housing facilitiy for a number of competitive sports. The Benny Leonard Arena is located there, a modern, state-of-the-art boxing center named for the great champion. On a wall in the arena is a large plaque which reads:

THIS FACILITY WAS MADE POSSIBLE
THROUGH THE GIFT OF A SINGLE DONOR
WHO WISHES TO REMAIN ANONYMOUS.
THE STATE OF ISRAEL AND THE ATHLETES
WHO WILL MAKE USE OF THIS ARENA
IN THE YEARS TO COME EXTEND THEIR
THANKS TO THIS BENEFACTOR, WHO,
BY HIS BEQUEST, HAS SHOWN THE SAME
SELFLESSNESS, GENEROSITY, AND LOVE FOR
THIS COUNTRY AND ITS PEOPLE
THAT WAS SO REPRESENTATIVE OF THE MAN
FOR WHOM THIS FACILITY IS NAMED.

JEWBOY

I

The sound of Winton Chalmers' gavel cracked through the courtroom as he lowered his considerable bulk into his chair. Before the gavel's echoes had faded, Ralph Markham, the defense attorney was on his feet.

"Your honor, I wish to renew my previous objection. The swastika is an ancient symbol found throughout Byzantine, Buddhist, Greek, and many American Indian cultures. My young client was merely exercising his First Amendment right of freedom of expression..."

"Put a sock in it and sit down, Mr. Markham. Unless you're prepared to tell this court that your client was practicing to be a Buddhist or a Byzantine or something, I don't want to hear it And as for the First Amendment, it says, as I recall, that Congress won't make any laws restricting freedom of speech. It doesn't say anything about freedom of expression, whatever that is. And in any event, I am neither the Congress, nor am I making any laws here. So the First Amendment doesn't apply. Besides, what Mr. Fishburn did...," (he gestured emphatically toward Exhibit A, a smeared and streaked can of Quick-'N-Easy Hi-Gloss black spray paint) "...was vandalism, pure and simple. If you think otherwise, you've got the right to appeal. But in the meantime, sit down and be quiet."

With a deliberately audible sigh, Attorney Markham dropped into his chair, leaned toward his client and whispered, "Sorry, kid, I did what I could for you."

"Sure," replied Larry Fishburn loud enough for everyone within earshot to hear. "Have you ever considered bagging burgers and fries for a living?"

"Quiet!" yelled the judge. "Young man, if you've got a problem with your attorney…"

"Yeah, I got a problem with him. And with you. And with this whole kangaroo court."

"Mr. Fishburn, you've been found guilty of vandalizing a place of worship. If you've got anything to say before I…"

"I got plenty to say." Larry bolted to his feet, nearly knocking his chair over backward. "I did what I did because this country is going to Hell. Why? Because the Jews are in charge of everything. The media, the banks, the courts, the government. You name it, the Jews run it. And who gets screwed? White people. You think I'm just some Halliwell loser, don't you? Maybe I am, but I know what's going on."

He had been addressing the bench, but now he half-turned to face the few spectators scattered about the room. His seventeen years of gradually accumulated frustration and rage boiled over into Judge Chalmers' court.

"Wake up!" he shrieked. "This used to be a great country. A <u>white</u> country. Now look at it. The border's being overrun by Mexicans, the niggers are breeding like rabbits, the Japs are flooding the universities, the Jews are running the whole show, and what do you do about it? You and the rest of White America, you sit in front of your TV with a six-pack and a bag of pretzels, while the greatest country in the history of the world goes down the toilet. Well, I'm not going down without a fight. When I decorated that kike-agogue, I was saying that there are still some white people out here who haven't got their heads in the sand, and who are gonna change things around. This time it was only paint. Next time…who knows?"

As he turned back to face the judge, a small, seated figure in the far corner of the room caught Larry Fishburn's eye. A man, perhaps twenty years old, whose black clothes, skull cap, beard, and elongated sideburns left no doubt as to his religion. His face was pale, almost chalky, and a scar that was even whiter than his complexion wound down from his brow, crossed his left eye, and extended halfway down his cheek. In contrast, his eyes were dark and oddly deep-set. No expression of any kind crossed his face, even when Larry Fishburn's eyes locked onto his.

"The time's coming, Jewboy." Larry called to the man and pointed at him. "The scales are gonna be squared, so enjoy the party while you can. Sieg heil."

And with that, his right arm snapped outward in a Nazi salute.

"I think I've heard enough," said the judge.

"I'll bet you have," Larry sneered. "How much are the local Yids paying you to railroad me?"

Ralph Markham grabbed hold of Larry's faded sport coat and hauled him down into the chair.

"What are you trying to do, you stupid...?" he hissed at Larry. "You want to be a martyr? You want to do time?"

"Where'd you study law, Moron U.? I'm under age, and it's my first offense. Even this Jew-loving judge can't give me jail time. Don't you know that?"

"Absolutely right, Mr. Fishburn," interrupted Judge Chalmers. "I can't impose incarceration for a first offense. The law is quite clear on that point."

Larry smiled smugly and cast a brief look of disdain and disgust at his lawyer.

"And," the judge continued, "the law states that if the punishment the court imposes is completed, on your eighteenth birthday this entire incident will be erased from your record. However,..."

Larry's smile drooped slightly.

"...the law does grant me considerable leeway in whatever punishment I choose to send your way. So here it is. Exactly two weeks from today, before the close of business at three o'clock, you will submit to me a research paper of no less than twenty pages, complete with footnotes and bibliography using at least six reputable sources. The subject of this paper will be antisemitism in the 20th century, and you're free to write on any aspect of this subject. The paper will be typed or word processed, not handwritten, and will follow the current composition standards utilized by the English department at your school."

As the judge spoke, Larry's smile trickled away. He turned to his lawyer. "Can he do this?"

"Indeed I can, Mr. Fishburn," the judge called out. "And if your paper is unsatisfactory in any way—in *any* way, I'm going to throw it out. If you copy from an encyclopedia or use five sources instead of six, even if your margins are too big, I'll rule that the conditions imposed by this court were not fulfilled, and your record will not be whitewashed. That can of paint over there will follow you for the rest of your life."

"Your honor!"

"What is it, Mr. Markham?"

"With all due respect, your field of expertise is not antisemitism or English composition. In all fairness I would ask that you…"

"I'm one step ahead of you, counselor. You're right. I wouldn't know how to properly grade a paper of this nature. That's why I've decided that the paper will be read and judged by someone other than me."

"Thank you, your honor," said Markham, managing a small smile. "Can you tell us who the reader will be?"

"Certainly. I've decided that your client's essay will be read and judged by Dr. Michael Szenes."

Larry snorted. "Who's he?"

The judge leaned forward, smiling, and riveted his eyes on Larry. "He's the rabbi of the synagogue you defaced."

Larry's jaw sagged open and Ralph Markham awkwardly scrambled to his feet to object. But Judge Chalmers' gavel was quicker, and it slammed onto the bench.

"This court is adjourned!"

II

Halliwell had once been considered a suburb of Philadelphia, separate and distinct. But over time, people began to think of it instead as the westernmost section of the city. Part of Philly proper. So the line that separated city from suburb slid further west, as did a lot of the professional people, as did the tax base, as did the ability to keep Halliwell High School current. HHS was not a bad school. The faculty and staff did the best with what they had; but over a not particularly long time, Halliwell High, though not a slum school, became most certainly a sad one.

Whenever budgetary problems force a school to tighten its belt, the library often seems to take the first (and frequently the hardest) hit. The library at HHS was a good example. The most recent encyclopedia on the shelf listed Jimmy Carter as the sitting president. The books were dusty since the janitorial staff had been cut to the bone and only got into the library every two or three weeks. Tables with decades of Halliwell names gouged into them told not only who had come before, but that no repair or replacement had come after. The radiators, when they worked, were noisy, the lighting was intermittent, the floors were dirty, and the librarian ill-trained.

It was Larry Fishburn's favorite place on earth.

He loved the quiet as well as the dirt and the sorry looking volumes that had been spread strategically around the room so as to give the impression that the collection was larger than it really was. Here he could read and think and be himself and not care what anyone else thought. He knew that even a poor excuse for a library like this one could still be a gold mine of ideas—popular ideas and not so popular ones. You just had to know where to look.

Best of all, there were days when, during his free periods, he was the only student to come through the library's doors. Seeing no one else in the room brought Larry as close to joy as he thought he'd ever come. It was all his. Every chair, table, book, magazine, and dust bunny. The Lawrence R. Fishburn Library. Admission by invitation only.

Larry had had few triumphs in his life, but here he could sit and replay them again and again. Especially how in ninth grade he had first heard about Adolph Hitler and racial superiority. And how he had made the class take notice of Larry Fishburn for the first time. Ms. Tallmadge's History 9 was doing a unit on World War II, and the text had mentioned Hitler's belief that white Germans were genetically superior to other people.

A hand went up.

"Yes, Larry."

"I've got a question." He cleared his throat and gestured toward the black students in the class, who always sat together. "No one can argue that these guys aren't superior to whites in a lot of sports. The NBA and the NFL are loaded with them. They jump higher, they run faster, they're more agile. Nobody disputes it. When was the last time a white guy won a gold medal in an Olympic sprint? They're better than we are. Period."

There was the sound of chuckling and slapped palms among the black students.

"Your point, please, Larry," Ms. Tallmadge said uneasily.

"My point is, isn't that evidence of racial superiority? Physical superiority. And if blacks are superior physically, why couldn't whites be superior mentally? Why couldn't Hitler have been right?"

The chuckling stopped.

Ms. Tallmadge tried to defuse the tension. She smiled slightly, trying to appear nonchalant.

"Larry, that's never been proven, and…"

"But could it be possible? Why can physical achievement be linked to race and not intellectual achievement?"

It was at this point that Larry usually stopped the movie in his head. He didn't remember how Ms. Tallmadge had responded. Weakly, no doubt. But he remembered the murmurs. Murmurs of anger and outrage and shock, to be sure. But there were some of agreement. He knew it. He felt it. By the end of the day, everybody had heard about what had happened in History 9.

Larry Fishburn had become somebody.

Soon afterward, a classified ad in the back of *Firearms Quarterly* had put Larry in touch with others who thought as he did, people who felt that the government was paying too much attention to gun owners who wanted to protect America and not enough to foreigners who wanted to pollute it. At last, Larry Fishburn, who had been in and out of foster homes since age 8, had a family. People who were genuinely pleased to communicate with him and exchange ideas. The fact that he was a kid and they were adults didn't seem to matter. In letters and phone conversation, his new friends wanted to hear his opinions, and told him how wonderful it was that one so young could think so maturely. They told him that he was in the forefront of a new movement, a movement that would take back the country from those who had despoiled it, and put right-thinking white Americans back in charge.

Larry not only had a family now.

He had a mission.

The memories made him feel better, as he sat forlornly at one of the beat-up library tables with a yellow pad and two encyclopedia volumes opened to entries on Judaism. The pad was blank. He had toyed with the idea of defying the judge. How about submitting a paper *defending* antisemitism? The judge had only told him to write on the subject. He hadn't said anything about which side of the issue to take. That'd shake up the fat fool for sure. On second thought, Larry remembered David Duke, who had been a leader in the Ku Klux Klan, but had traded in his sheet and hood for a suit and a briefcase, and had run for Congress from Louisiana and won. Larry figured that if he wanted to make a difference in the future, he'd be better off with a clean record. That meant swallowing his pride and doing what the judge ordered.

But where to start? The paper was going nowhere.

It was then that Larry looked across the empty library and saw the Jew. The one who'd been in the courtroom during the trial. He was sitting rigidly at an empty table off to the side, staring, not in Larry's direction, but straight ahead into space.

Larry's breath hitched, and a shot of adrenaline made his heart pound. He jumped to his feet, knocking his chair over with a crash, but the Jew's unblinking gaze didn't change. The same ashen face. The same fixed eyes. What was he looking at? Anything? Maybe he was in some kind of trance? You never can tell about some of these weird religions. But what to do? Larry's first instinct was to confront the intruder himself,

getthehellouttamylibrary

but instead he figured, "Why not let the system do something constructive for a change." He walked to the circulation desk where the librarian was sorting cards.

"Mrs. Hammond?"

She looked up and smiled at her most loyal patron.

"Yes, Larry."

"Isn't it a school policy that only Halliwell students can use the library?"

"Yes, that's so."

"Well," said Larry jerking his thumb over his shoulder, "he doesn't go to school here."

"Who doesn't?"

"Him." Larry half-turned and pointed to the table. The chairs were all neatly in place.

And the Jew was gone.

"Where'd…? He was sitting right there."

"Larry, no one's been here this morning except you."

"I saw him!" Larry yelled. He stormed over to the table. "He was in this chair ten seconds ago. This chair. He must have run out, or something"

Mrs. Hammond sighed, came out from behind the desk, and walked to the library door.

"This is the only way in or out of here."

"Yeah? So?"

She looked at Larry as she pulled the door open. The old hinges screeched.

Larry got the point. No one could have gone through that door without advertising it.

As Mrs. Hammond went back to her post behind the desk, Larry stood where he was and tried to rationalize what he'd seen.

"I know he was here," he muttered to himself. "Either that, or I'm losing it." He stalked back to his table, righted his chair, sat down for about a millisecond, and then shot back up to his feet as if he'd sat on a snake. On his yellow pad, his blank yellow pad, someone had scrawled in a crabbed, ragged hand

CAN HELP. 4117 THIRD AVE. 8PM. THIS NIGHT ONLY

III

Normally, Larry wouldn't have bothered. It was cold, Third Avenue was at least a mile from his house, and he had homework to do, not to mention another day had gone by and he hadn't written a word for the Hanging Judge. But there was something bubbling in his gut. Larry was used to rattling other people, not being the rattlee. And much as he hated to admit it, the writing on the pad had really shaken him. The only thing to do was to get in the Jew's face and let whatever happened happen.

"Okay, so he spooked me." Larry thought out loud, as he trudged along. "Bad move, Jewboy. Major bad move." He smacked a fist into a palm, and flexed his fingers. Both hands were wrapped with gauze and duct tape with a tape seam running across his knuckles. Hands are fragile, and can easily break in a fight unless properly wrapped to keep the bones from moving around. More power, less injury. A win-win situation. And the seam made facial cuts open nicely. A bonus.

Larry was ready.

"An animal's most dangerous when it's been hurt or caught unawares. It's nature." He drew his hands under his chin, and threw a series of jabs and uppercuts into the air. The chill of the air cold-burned the inside of his nose, but he relished the sting. "It's nature. That which does not kill me, makes me stronger," he hissed between punches. "German philosophy, of course."

Larry liked autumn, the way it looked, the way it smelled. And as he headed toward his confrontation with the Jew, Larry felt the rush of elation that accompanies the feeling that you can't lose. That you have a sure thing going. Jews don't fight. It's a fact. This was going to be a coast.

He crossed First Avenue where the nice houses were, and Second Avenue where the so-so houses were, and headed for Third Avenue where the not-so-nice houses were. "Weird," he thought. "A Jew living on Third. Must have his money stuffed in his mattress." A thought flickered in Larry's mind for an instant, but he quickly snuffed it out with a sneer. "I'm no thief," he said, assuring himself of his moral superiority. "Just take care of business." And he snapped a double jab-straight right combination into the night.

He turned onto Third Avenue and tried to get his bearings in the dark. When streetlights had come to Halliwell, however many years ago, by the time the poles were due to be installed on Third, the money well had run dry. So here it was years later, and still no lights. No matter. The dark was Larry's ally. He did most of his best work in the dark. He smiled with the assurance of a poker player holding a royal flush. Everything that could go right, was.

Eventually he found the house, a small bungalow tucked between a warehouse and a 24-hour laundromat that had the inside of its windows soaped and the word CLOSED traced in the soap. The house was dark except for a faint flicker of light coming through one of the front windows. Or maybe some feeble light source was reflecting on the window from out in the street. Larry wasn't sure. He squinted through the darkness. Four wooden steps led up to a tiny porch.

The front door was half open.

He swallowed even though there was no spit in his mouth, and, for the first time, the chill of the air sent a short shiver through him. A trap. Had to be. Nobody but a fool would leave a Third Avenue door unlocked, much less open. Larry noticed that his breathing had become shallower and more rapid. He flexed his hands against the gauze and tape. "Okay, Jewboy. I'll play." Without a sound, and with every nerve ending ready to fire, Larry slowly made his way toward the narrow steps. His ears were on edge, straining to receive any information they could pass on to his brain. Night noises he hadn't noticed before seemed to hammer his ears. Alley cats, distant car engines, boombox music even though filtered through closed windows—all appeared to be conspiring to mask any sounds that might come from within the house. But there was no sound near him except the wind-blown leaves scratching across the pavement in the dark.

He carefully walked up the left side of the stairs. Wooden steps are generally nailed down near the ends of the boards, so if you put your feet there, there's less chance of a squeak. At the top of the stairs, he flattened himself back against the house next to the open door. Slowly, silently, he slipped through the doorway.

The flickering he had seen from the street was indeed coming from inside, from the room off to his right. "Moth to a flame," he thought as he peered around the corner.

The room was a rectangle about thirty feet long, and empty except for a small kitchen-size table at the far end. A thick, stubby candle set in the center of the table sputtered, sending crazy shapes undulating across the walls.

The Jew sat at the table with his back to Larry. As in the library, he was rigidly upright, hands resting on the tabletop, and totally without motion. Like a mannequin.

Larry ran a number of courses of action through his mind before he decided to yell and scare the daylights out of the Jew. As he opened his mouth, an old, grating, raspy voice came from the Jew's direction.

"I hoped you would come," it said.

Larry forced himself to ignore the eeriness of the voice. "Listen, Jewboy," he bellowed, "I don't need anything from you. Keep the hell away from me, and keep the hell out of my library. Got it?"

Silence. The Jew didn't budge.

Larry took two threatening steps forward. "I'm talking to you."

"Have you injured your hands?" the voice asked haltingly.

Larry's jaw grew slack and his knees buckled momentarily. There was no way the Jew could have seen his wrapped hands. "How did…?"

"I know much of you, Mr. Fishburn, and yet I know nothing of you."

"What're you talking about? You don't know me."

"You or those like you. It makes no difference."

"What are you talking about?"

"You hate me, don't you?"

"Damn straight," said Larry. He was pleased that the confrontation seemed at last to be swinging into comfortable territory, but he was still unnerved at having to talk to the Jew's back. "This country's going to hell because of you and your kind."

"You hate me without knowing me."

Larry tossed off one of his favorite lines. "I don't need to know about a disease to have it kill me."

"And yet, a vaccine which can protect you from a disease must introduce a small amount of the disease into your system. Thus, the disease which can kill you can also make you stronger."

"*That which does not kill me…*" It was like the Jew could peer into Larry's brain.

"That's it, Jewboy." Larry stalked toward the seated figure, and, when he was close enough, uncorked a looping right that would have pulverized most of the bones in the Jew's face.

If it had landed.

Milliseconds before impact, the Jew's right hand shot up, as if it had its own set of eyes, and caught Larry's fist as casually as a center fielder would snag an easy fly ball.

As the absurdity of the situation settled in (*Jews don't fight…it's a fact*), Larry's brain refused to accept the knowledge that, with the exception of the arm and hand, the Jew's body had remained as it was— eyes staring ahead, body immobile. Larry's punch hadn't budged the man an inch.

But the fear didn't set in until he realized that his hand was caught. The Jew's fingers had encased Larry's fist in a frighteningly powerful grip, and Larry futiley tried to pry the dry, leathery fingers off with his other hand. They wouldn't move, and fear gave way to panic. His brain tried to camouflage the real danger of his predicament by sending long lost memories coursing through his consciousness. He remembered when he was little, how he'd read the story of Bre'r Rabbit and the Tar Baby, and of how the supposedly clever rabbit had stupidly got himself

caught. The memory was not a comfort. Grunting, whimpering, Larry frenziedly tried to yank himself free, thrashing about like a fish on a hook.

The Jew, still motionless, still staring at the wall, spoke in that gravelly monotone that sounded much older than he appeared to be.

"I will help you, Mr. Fishburn."

"I don't want your help," Larry squealed. He refused to beg the Jew to let him go, but he was fast approaching that level of desperation.

"Nonetheless, it must be given you." And with that, the Jew slowly and effortlessly pulled Larry around, forcing his shoulders onto the table.

"Leave me alone," Larry bawled. "I won't bother you anymore. For God's sake, leave me alone."

"I cannot, Mr. Fishburn," the voice answered. Mechanically, the Jew turned his head and looked blankly, squarely down into Larry's terrified face. "I cannot."

Larry had never screamed before in his life. But he did now. Not because he was trapped. Not because the Jew's face with its sunken eyes and crusty skin looked like something that didn't belong above ground. Not because the scar that wound itself down the Jew's face seemed to be glowing, pulsing, as if it had a life of its own. But because as the Jew spoke, his ashen lips never parted, his mouth never opened. There was no way that awful voice could escape its body. And yet Larry heard every word. Until his screams drowned the words out. Again and again. Breath after breath was sucked in and squeezed back out in shrieks that Larry knew were probably paving a road to madness.

And then it was gone. The terror that held him every bit as tightly as the Jew's hand dissipated, and was replaced by a soft, warm peace as strength and will oozed from Larry's body and mind. Total paralysis had set in, and Larry realized that the Jew could do whatever he pleased. It was the calm that resignation brings, and Larry not-too-reluctantly welcomed it. The Jew knew what Larry was feeling.

"No, Mr. Fishburn, you will not die tonight. Not tonight."

The voice had not changed, but it was no longer frightening. In fact, it was almost soothing. Comforting.

"Who are you?" he asked weakly.

"I am Yosef Polanski. I have come to help you." And with that he hauled Larry's limp body onto the table, knocking over the candle. The flame licked the Jew's hand causing the flesh to sizzle, and the smell to fill Larry's nostrils, but the Jew seemed not to notice.

"Please, don't," Larry whispered.

"You profess to be a seeker of truth, Mr. Fishburn. Tonight, you will see and experience Truth. And you will survive Truth. What you will do afterward is not for me to say, but for you to live."

The hard surface under Larry's back grew softer and softer, and he felt himself slowly sinking into it as if it were quicksand. Powerless, he saw Yosef Polanski fading upward into distance, as thick blackness rose up around him like the sides of a deep well.

"Remember what you see, Mr. Fishburn."

The voice was barely audible, soft with reverberation as Larry sank into oblivion.

"Remember what you see."

III

Even before he opened his eyes, Larry noticed the freshness of the air. It was sweet and clean and cool. He was still on his back, but he felt pebbles under his shoulders and dirt under his hands which weren't wrapped anymore. Even with his eyes closed he knew it was daylight. Slowly, he cracked one eyelid allowing a sliver of sun in, but it was too much and he flopped an arm flopped across his eyes, and he rolled over into weeds.

"There's no weeds on Third," his brain told him. But before he had time to think further, he felt the vibration, a low, steady rumble that passed softly through his body.

Quickly, gradually, the vibration grew stronger until the continuous rumble began to disintegrate into hundreds of small, soft and progressively harsher leaden thuds. It reminded him of a newspaper photo that appeared solid until you looked closely and saw it was made of countless tiny ink dots. There was something familiar about the sound, and Larry's mind groped for a reference.

"Cowboys and Indians," he thought. He suddenly knew the sound.

He struggled to open his eyes and get to his feet at the same time. The eyes opened, but the legs gave way, and he sank to his haunches.

The collapse probably saved his life.

As he fell, and some ten or fifteen horsemen raced furiously by him, something cracked across the top of his head, something hard and (the clang that reverberated through his skull told him) metallic. He toppled over with blood trickling into his eyes. Voices howled and hooted, and Larry looked vacantly at the men. They were carrying clubs, mallets, lengths of chain—an assortment of things. The one whose lead pipe was streaked with Larry's blood spat and cursed in a strange language that Larry somehow understood. The man's riding companions laughed. "Yevgeny, you fool. If you wouldn't drink so much your aim would be better."

The man with the pipe sputtered something, but his friends were unanimous. "You only get credit for a direct hit. Next time aim lower." And they all disappeared down the road in a billow of dust and raucous voices.

"You said I wouldn't die," Larry's mind whispered. The fact that he didn't know where he was and didn't know who had assaulted him or why wasn't important now. It was time to go gently.

"You shall not die, Mr. Fishburn," said a raspy voice in his brain. "Though you will see things to make you wish you had."

"Leave me alone."

"I cannot!"

Larry's body rose slowly and tentatively from the ground. It was then that he realized that the body wasn't his. The hands had stubby, callused fingers. An ample belly hid the top of the belt, and two well-bowed legs moved the wounded body down the road in the direction the horsemen had ridden. As he shambled along with a rickety, stumbling gait, Larry realized that the body was moving of its own accord and that he was trapped inside, like a passenger in the back seat of an out-of-control police car.

Larry tried to cry out, but there was no voice connected to his brain. All he had was thought.

"Don't be afraid, Mr. Fishburn," the voice of Yosef Polanski reassured him "You are here only to witness, not to act."

"Where…?"

"You are in the Ukraine. It is 1903, and the man inside whom you are, is trying to reach his home. His name is Aaron Glantzer. He was walking home from the next town when he stopped to rest. He's from a small town called Kishinev, a short distance away. His wife is there, and he knows that the horsemen will arrive any moment."

"Who are they?" Larry thought as he watched the road jerkily slip by under the feet.

"Local hooligans hired by the regional government. Life has always been hard here, and new ideas are being whispered, ideas of freedom and revolution. Of brotherhood and bread. The authorities fear these ideas, and so they deflect criticism by blaming and beating those who are weak and without political power."

"Jews, I suppose?" Larry thought, managing a mental sneer.

"Yes. A new word has been coined to describe what is about to happen. Pogrom."

"If a few people get beat up, so what? What do you expect me to do about it?"

The edge of the town appeared through Aaron Glantzer's eyes. There was smoke. And screaming. His stocky legs tried to accelerate but his wheezing lungs had little oxygen to send.

"Nothing is expected of you, Mr. Fishburn, because nothing is possible. Your mind is suspended in the mind of this man. You will watch through his eyes. You will hear and see as he does. But you are incapable of any response. Your only obligation here is to witness."

And he did. He watched as the horsemen rode down anyone they saw. Skulls were crushed and bodies bloodied as the horses trampled a gruesome swath through the center of the town. Within minutes, the street was littered with the dead, the dying, and those pretending to be dead, hoping that death might be fooled, and pass them by. Soon the men tired of their sport and, realizing they could accomplish only so much on horseback, dismounted. It had been a long ride to Kishinev, so while a few of the men watered and tended the animals, the rest went from house to house continuing their work.

Aaron Glantzer was smart enough to keep out of sight. He zig-zagged his way around and between the ramshackle buildings, ducking beneath windows and sliding past doors, trying to ignore the screams of his neighbors that seemed to be coming from everywhere. He pressed himself flat against the side of one house just as the front door flew open and three Ukrainians emerged. One dragged a half-dressed young woman by the hair, the second held an infant upside-down, it's tiny foot buried in the man's hand, and the third backed out of the house with a torch, spreading fire evenly and generously throughout the small structure.

"Hey, Jew," said the one holding the woman's hair. "If you want to go to America someday, you have to know American games. I like soccer." He smiled as he unleashed a fearsome kick to her ribs. The sound of the snapping bones made him chuckle. "But in America they have baseball. I don't know baseball." He brought his face next to hers and smiled as she struggled to draw air into her lungs and, at the same time, feebly held her arms out to her child. "Do you know baseball, Jew?" He called to the man holding the baby. "Nicki, we show this Jew baseball."

Knowing she could barely move, he released her hair, strode to her fence, and kicked and pried a wide slat free. The woman tried to haul her body across the dirt toward her child, but only managed to cover a foot or two before the man returned. With the board resting over his shoulder, he shoved the woman to her back with his boot, and cheerfully called to his comrade, "Throw the ball, Nicki. I will hit home run." The woman's mouth opened freakishly wide, but no sound emerged. Nicki flung the baby and the man swung the board.

Larry was glad that Aaron Glantzer could no longer watch. But the whack of the board came through clearly, as did the soft thud of a tiny body landing in the street, and the hooting sounds of men at play.

Aaron Glantzer reached his small home just ahead of the marauders. He found his wife cowering inside and gathered her up for a run across the marsh fields. He knew that the fields were pockmarked with animal burrows, uneven terrain, and patches of ground too soft to support much weight. Many legs and ankles had been twisted or broken by people and animals who had attempted to run across the expanse. Aaron Glantzer knew his way, knew where the ground was flat and solid, knew how to get across quickly. But as he stuffed the photo of his older brother who had gone to America inside his shirt, the door splintered inward and three men began calling "Come out, Jews. Time for synagogue. Time for prayers."

The first one through the door carried a blood-smeared length of lead pipe. When Aaron Glantzer saw him, rage bulled fear aside, and he roared forward knocking the one they had called Yevgeny backward through the door frame, into his two companions. The pipe was wrenched from the man's hand, and Aaron Glantzer began swinging wildly, like Samson smiting the Philistines. He bludgeoned two of the thugs and was advancing on the third when a bullet ripped into his thigh, and with a gurgling bellow he went sprawling.

Larry saw all of this and had to admit a grudging admiration for Aaron Glantzer who, even with his leg blown open and his skull fractured, was still full of fight as he struggled to right himself using the pipe as a crutch.

A man approached casually on horseback, his smoking pistol held aloft. Behind him, his men had rounded up nearly thirty Kishinevers and were marching them en masse toward the center of town. Toward the synagogue.

"Get him to his feet," the man said pointing to Aaron. Two of Aaron's neighbors hoisted him upright, and with his wife clutching his shirttail, they joined the march.

The Kishinev synagogue was a large wooden building whose size was the only thing that distinguished it from the other drab structures that surrounded it. The Jews were herded inside as the Ukranians called out "Time for prayers, Jews. Time for prayers." Once the people were inside, the doors were shut from the outside, ropes tied across the handles, and boards nailed across the doorframes and windows. As the synagogue was set afire, the men outside passed around bottles of vodka, and sang songs about home and family and friendship and the motherland.

Each of those inside marked the coming of death in his or her own way. Some cried. Some prayed. Some hurled their bodies uselessly against the doors, and others tried to claw holes in the walls. A few sat motionless, wrapped in soft blankets of numbness their minds had mercifully pulled up around them. The air was full of smoke and screams and "Shema Yisroeyl." Many cursed God and said the Torah was a lie and the mitzvot a fraud. But Aaron Glantzer held his wife to his wide chest and whispered just loud enough for her to hear, "I cannot curse a God who has given me such a woman, if only for a time." He lifted her face in his bloody hands. "Malka," he said, "I die the happiest of men."

Larry watched, more caught up in Aaron Glantzer's tearless eloquence than in the chaos and the din that assaulted what senses he had.

"He will die here with all of them and be forgotten," said the voice of Yosef Polanski. "No one will know that his heart ever beat or that he loved his wife or that he couldn't sing but still loved the songs of his people. No one will know how much he wanted a son, but how much he cherished the daughter whom he named for his mother and whose life ended less than a day after it began. Dying like this is one thing, Mr. Fishburn. But being forgotten is like never having existed."

Aaron Glantzer pulled his Malka tight to him and kissed her hair, just as the roof collapsed.

IV

The darkness came abruptly, but the quiet crept in like a mouse nosing about for food in a strange room. Larry didn't know how much time had passed, but the first tendrils of claustrophobic panic began to wind their way into his brain.

"Hey!" his mind called out.

"Don't be afraid, Mr. Fishburn," said the voice of Yosef Polanski.

"I'm not afraid and I'm not impressed," Larry replied calmly, packing two considerable lies into a single thought.

"I'm glad, Mr. Fishburn, because this episode will probably not be the worst thing you will see tonight."

"What's your point?"

"I have no point other than to show you things of which you may not be aware, and…"

"And hope that all this will make me l-o-o-o-v-e Jews, right? You think this is going to change my mind about you people?""

"No one can change your mind about anything without your consent, Mr. Fishburn."

"Damn straight. You guys are so good at making the rest of the world feel guilty about your problems. Oh, those poor, poor Jews. I'm not going to take the blame for what a bunch of drunken Cossacks did a hundred years ago. I wasn't there. I wasn't responsible. I don't even care. What they did is over and done. Finished."

"But the beast that caused it is still alive, still hungry, and you keep it well fed."

"No!" shouted Larry's mind. "You're not going to pin what those guys did on me. I'm an American, not some stupid peasant. I'm an American. You got that?"

"Yes," said the voice growing noticeably fainter. "An American…An American…"

V

Even with his eyes tightly closed, Larry knew that some unit of time had passed—hour, day, century—something, even though he was sure that on Third Avenue in Halliwell, P. A. it was still the same night it had been when he'd begun this insane odyssey. He cracked one eye and could make out a single dimly lit bulb dangling from the ceiling—but it wasn't the ceiling on Third Avenue. Larry figured it would be easier to think and get his initial bearings without visual distraction, so the eye sagged shut, and his senses opened wide. His ears told him nothing. Silence. His nose inhaled air heavy with the smell of mold and human waste. His hands felt a mattress not much thicker than a blanket on a metal frame. A cot.

He opened both eyes. The light from the bulb, though feeble, still made him squint. The thought of a baby being thrust into the glare of a delivery room skipped across his mind.

hey Nicki we show this Jew baseball

He turned his head to the right and scraped his nose on a concrete block wall.

"Damn!" He drew his hands up to his wounded face. The hands weren't those of Aaron Glantzer.

But they weren't Larry Fishburn's, either.

As he sat up on the edge of the cot, the old springs popped and pinged. He touched his nose, and a bolt of pain ricocheted through his skull. "Jesus," he croaked to no one in particular.

A voice rolled in from the next room. "You got a problem in there, Jewboy?" Larry turned his head toward the voice and saw bars. He was in a small cell, empty but for the cot, a sink with a single faucet and a five gallon bucket obviously meant to be used as a toilet. A well lit doorway led into an adjoining room. The voice had come from there.

"Why doncha just go back to sleep?" said the voice. A second voice piped up. "Yeah. Dream about Mary, why doncha, ya sick bastard." This last was followed by poorly muffled snorts.

"Great," Larry muttered as he stood up. And it dawned on him that he had wanted to stand, and he had stood. He was in control of whosever body this was. "That's a plus," he thought sarcastically as he walked to the sink and turned the faucet handle, all the while forcing himself to avoid looking in the bucket.

Nothing came from the spigot but a sigh of stale air.

"How about a drink?" he managed to croak.

Mumbles and giggles from the next room. "Sure, Jewboy." Within seconds, a large shape filled the doorway blocking out most of the adjoining light. As the shape drew closer, Larry could see a shock of curly red hair, wide shoulders, an even wider waistline, and a bulging cheek that told Larry that the guy must have a chunk of tobacco the size of a golf ball in his mouth. The guard smiled idiotically, and slipped a beefy hand holding a glass of water through the bars. "Here ya go." As Larry reached for it, the guard jerked his hand back through the bars, spit a large glob of tobacco juice into the glass, and re-offered it to Larry .

"Thought I'd give it a little flavor for ya."

Larry stared blankly at the guard.

"What's the matter, Jewboy? Thought you was thirsty." A good-ol'-boy grin stretched across the guard's face. He was obviously enjoying himself. "Oh, no," he cried out in mock horror. "This water ain't kosher no more!" He called back over his shoulder, "Hey, Ray. He cain't drink this water. It ain't kosher. What'll we do?" From the next room came a snort and a reply. "There's always the bucket."

"Now, Ray, we don't know that what's in the bucket's kosher."

"Why not? It came out of a genuine (he pronounced it jen-you-wine) New York City Jew. Cain't get any kosherer than that."

"I believe you're right, Ray." The cop jiggled the glass slightly like a dog-catcher waggling a bone to coax a stray into the pound-wagon. "What'll it be, Jewboy?"

Larry didn't move, but continued to stare incredulously at the fat guard.

"Ah, hell," the man grunted, as he flicked the contents of the glass into Larry's face, and walked out.

Larry's whole body shook with rage and disgust and humiliation. A comment about the guard's mother struggled to escape from behind his clenched teeth, but, knowing what the guard could and probably would do to him, he kept it to himself.

"August 17, 1915, Mr. Fishburn," said the voice of Yosef Polanski.

"Huh?" Larry had been so fixated on the guard that he was startled by the voice.

"Georgia, USA. America."

Larry took a second to move his emotional joystick from fear to bravado. "Great. So now what?"

"Your name is Leo Frank. Two years ago you were accused and found guilty of the murder of a girl who worked in your factory in Atlanta."

"Don't tell me. The poor Jew is convicted of something he didn't do and the government fries him in the electric chair or something. Is that about right?"

107

Yosef Polanski's voice continued. "Earlier today, the governor commuted your sentence...."

"It's not *my* sentence," Larry snapped. "*I* didn't do anything."

From the next room one of the guards barked, "Shut up in there, ya creep.."

"...from death to life imprisonment. At this moment you're awaiting transfer to the state penitentiary to begin serving your sentence."

"Is there a point to this?"

"Yes. Even in a racist time like this, a jury was willing to accept the perjured testimony of a black man over the truthful testimony of a Jew. In 1983, an eyewitness who is only a frightened boy today will finally come forward and admit that you were innocent."

"A miscarriage of justice. Breaks my heart."

"In 1986, the State of Georgia will issue you a full pardon. Posthumously, of course."

"You think this Jew is the only guy who ever pulled down time for something he didn't do? Wake up." Larry stretched out on his cot trying to ignore the dryness in his throat and the queasiness in his stomach. He hadn't noticed how really foul the stench in the cell was. But now his nose tingled from the odor, and he cupped both hands over his face hoping that air strained through his fingers might be a little less disgusting.

It wasn't.

"An innocent man goes to jail in Crackerville, USA," he muttered. I don't know why you're surprised. I'm not."

"Patience, Mr. Fishburn."

"Where are you, anyway? In my head? In outer space? Where?"

"Does it matter?"

"Do Jews have something against giving a straight answer?"

"No. But at times the question asked can't be answered simply. Where I am is not important. What is important is about to happen outside your window."

Larry hauled himself upright and peered through the bars into the thick Georgia night just as five Model T's (1915, he reminded himself) careened into view and pulled up in front of the prison gate. At least two dozen men sprang from the cars, and with the precision of a police SWAT team, went to work. Two of them sprinted to a nearby telephone pole, and while one held a lantern, the other shinnied up the pole with a set of bolt-cutters and severed the wires. The gatekeeper tried to run for help, but changed his mind when he heard "freeze," followed by the cocking of a double-barreled pump shotgun.

Larry watched in bemused fascination as the men raced through the gate, split up into smaller groups, and headed off to different parts of the prison compound. A contingent of five headed toward his cellblock.

Larry suddenly knew what was about to happen to him. He jumped to the bars of his cell and called out to the guards just as the night riders burst through the outer door. They overpowered the guards, grabbed the keys, and scrambled into the cell row.

"Look, there he is." The din that had accompanied them into the row vanished. They froze in their tracks, staring silently at Larry like kids ogling a two-headed calf at the county fair.

"It *is* him," another of the men said in an awed voice barely above a whisper. "I thought he'd be bigger."

"We've got a job to do," said another of the men, breaking the spell. The door to Larry's cell flew open, and he fell back onto his cot, kicking and flailing frantically at the hands that clutched for him. They bound his hands with adhesive tape, and dragged him from the cell, squirming and writhing.

"Slippery little bugger, ain't ya, Jewboy," said the man holding one of Larry's arms. "What say we make this easier," and the back of his hand smashed into Larry's face, breaking his nose, and causing his body to go limp. "I think that's better, don't you?"

They bundled Larry out past the guards who had been trussed up, and stuffed him between two men in the back seat of one of the idling cars.

"Hit it, Jim," cried one of the men to the driver, who floorboarded the pedal, spraying a cloud of cinders behind them. The men in the car whooped their satisfaction. The entire operation had taken only five minutes.

For the next several hours, the car jostled over miles of packed clay. The frenzy and euphoria of the raid faded surprisingly quickly, and as the car rolled through four counties toward Marietta, the hometown of Mary Phagan, the dead girl, the silence in the car was broken only when the driver occasionally asked his companions for directions.

As dawn broke over the horizon, Larry was able to see the men clearly. Well-groomed mustaches. Clean clothes. Wing-tip shoes and pocket watches. The car was new. No surprise there—the smell of a new car is unmistakable. But the air in the car, even with the windows down, had also been filled with the sweet scent of cologne, barber's talc and hair tonic.

The man on Larry's left leaned forward, eyeing the landscape from over the driver's shoulder. "There's a cutoff around here somewheres." Eyes scanned the scrub lining both sides of the road.

"I see it," said the driver pointing to a break in the brush.

"Okay, swing up there."

As the procession wound up a small hill, in the near distance Larry could see Marietta, quiet and pretty, nestled gently in the valley. The car's gears meshed smoothly with barely a sound or a hitch, as the driver made his way to the top.

"What say we help Jim wash this buggy down when we're through?" said one of the men.

"If we don't, Edie's gonna give *him* a cleaning when he gets home," said another.

Jim smiled, and the car filled with tired, fraternal laughter.

At the top of the hill, the cars pulled up to a group of trees—maples, Larry thought.

The car doors opened, and the men stepped out, stretching, yawning, and tugging at sweaty clothes. One reached in and took hold of Larry's sleeve saying "Let's go." Larry jerked himself back. The man reached in again, this time grabbing Larry's collar with one hand and a handful of hair with the other. "Nothing personal," he hissed, "But if you don't get out right now, so help me I'll break your damn neck."

Another of the men call out, "Need any help, Clayt?"

"You do your job, and I'll do mine," Clayt called sharply over his shoulder. He turned back to Larry. "What's it gonna be?"

Yosef Polanski's voice sounded in Larry's head. "You cannot change history, Mr. Fishburn. Though you control the body, you cannot alter what is to be. Leo Frank will die, but you will be safe."

As he was pulled whimpering from the car, something that Clayt had said replayed in Larry's mind. "Nothing personal," he'd said. And Larry knew the man was probably telling the truth. During the nightlong ride, they hadn't abused him physically or verbally. The quiet in the car had been the introspective quiet of men with a mission. In their minds, this was not a personal vendetta. They believed that Georgia justice had somehow been thwarted by this New York Jew, and by God, they were going to put things back in balance.

The scales of right had tipped out of whack, and they were going to square the scales.

They weren't a lynch mob. Oh no, they were good citizens righting a wrong, correcting a glitch in the system. Nothing more, nothing less. Mary Phagan's death would be avenged within eyeshot of her hometown.

Clayt hauled Larry over to a tree. A long, heavy hemp rope with a noose tied on one end was tossed over a low branch, and the noose pulled over Larry's head.

He began to cry. Softly. But his body shook with the terror that only comes when death is imminent.

"Stop it," Clayt said firmly but without anger. "You've acted like a man 'til now. See it through."

"But I'm not the guy," Larry bawled. "I'm not him."

"Leo Frank," Clayt announced in a voice loud enough for all to hear, "you've been found guilty by the State of Georgia, and sentenced to die."

"But the governor…"

"We'll take care of him later. The sentence will now be carried out."

"But I'm not the guy! I'm not a Jew!"

"Haul him up, boys."

A scream had barely escaped Larry's throat when it was choked into a gurgle. He felt himself rising but didn't feel like he was being pulled. He was floating. High. Very high. Too high. He looked down and saw the ground slowly dropping away. Below him, Leo Frank's body was convulsing and kicking in its death throes.

"Observe, Mr. Fishburn," said the voice of Yosef Polanski. "The terror is done…"

As Larry rose higher, he saw the men pile into their cars amid patted backs and shaken hands, and slowly drive from the scene.

"…but now the horror begins."

Within minutes a crowd began to form. From all sides of the hill they came, from Marietta and from neighboring towns. The numbers swelled until over a thousand people, men, women, and children had massed on the hill to gawk at the gently swaying body of Leo Frank. Men held their children overhead so they could see better. Some brought breakfast. Occasionally, there was applause.

Larry felt himself continuing upward. Details on the ground were becoming harder to make out, but he noticed sharp flashes of light around the base of the tree.

"Flashbulbs, Mr. Fishburn. Families, friends, couples, children. All having their pictures taken at the feet of the dead Jew. Throughout the state, pictures of Leo Frank's hanging body surrounded by smiling people will grace penny postcards and souvenir photo albums . People not here will claim to have witnessed the event, and their friends will nod in envy and admiration. When the body is taken down by a town official, its face will be kicked in by a local citizen who felt the corpse didn't warrant an autopsy and burial, but should instead be burned. A new governor will offer a reward for the arrest and capture of the perpetrators…five hundred dollars…for all twenty-five men. Twenty dollars per man. Of course, no one will ever be named or caught or tried."

As the pops of light became fainter and farther away, they began to resemble fireflies.

"I can't change who I am," he thought.

"On the contrary, you're the *only* one who can change who you are."

Larry's brain was teetering on the edge of consciousness. As clouds began to obscure the ground, he was aware that his upward movement was slowing. Soon it stopped. For a time he felt like he was

suspended in milk. But the voice of Yosef Polanski continued unabated, emotionless and monotonic.

"Still you have not seen the worst. Those people below. Ordinary people. Simple, uneducated people. They take pride in who they are, and distrust those who are different. Perhaps they are not intellectually or culturally advanced. So let us see, Mr. Fishburn. Let us see what an advanced society can do. Let us look at the people you most revere."

Without warning, Larry began to fall back through the clouds. Faster and faster. Terminal velocity. He opened his mouth but the wind stuffed any sound back into his throat. He saw the ground and a complex of low, long buildings hurtling, spinning up toward him. The ground was green. "It's not Georgia," he thought as his mind went dark.

VI

way uh house…way uh…

The voice was soft and distant. Larry could barely hear it.

way uh house

A hand grabbed Larry's shoulder and shook him roughly.

(nothingpersonalbutifyoudontgetoutrightnow…)

Larry's eyes snapped open and his body went rigid as if he'd grabbed a live wire.

"Wake up, Klaus. Come on. You'll be late."

Larry flopped back onto his pillow, panting.

"You'd better get moving. It's Friday."

"Huh?" Larry turned to the man who'd wakened him. Young. Blonde. Unsmiling.

And wearing the uniform of a German officer.

"Friday? Barracks 9 duty? Remember?"

Larry looked at him blankly. He rapped his knuckles on Larry's head.

"HELLO! IS ANYONE IN THERE?"

Larry swept the hand away and slowly sat up on the cot. The officer walked to his own bed and resumed shining his boots. Larry stood up, stretched, yawned, and looked around. Two rows of beds in the center of the room, and a row of large clothes lockers on each of the side walls. In the center of the rear end wall hung a six foot square portrait of Adolph Hitler. To its left, a Nazi flag. To its right, a large map bearing the legend "Dachau Resettlement Camp - 1943."

"Fifteen minutes," said the officer.

"Huh?"

"Is that all you can say? 'Huh? Huh?'"

"Um…" He couldn't take his eyes off the man's uniform.

"Don't tax your brain, Klaus. We've got fifteen minutes to get to 9. Better move. If you're late

118

again…Well, let's just say the doctor won't be pleased. And I'm not waiting for you this time."

Larry looked around, saw the door to the shower room, and staggered off.

"Hey!" called his neighbor.

"Huh?"

"Forget something?"

Larry stared stupidly at him.

"SOAP? TOWEL? Come on, Klaus, wake up!"

"Right." He shambled back to his cot, opened the footlocker, grabbed a towel and soap and walked quickly to the shower. The water was warm and clean, and he felt better than he had since he'd begun his ridiculous ordeal eons ago. He towelled off and hustled back to the footlocker, only to realize that Klaus's uniform was probably hanging in one of the clothes lockers against the wall. But which one? There were no names on the doors. And even if he found the right one, he wouldn't know the combination to the padlock. The other man was buffing his boots, beating a steady rhythm with the brush as he kept an eye on Larry. Larry looked back at him, smiled sheepishly, and began turning the dial on the nearest lock. His plan worked.

"Hey," yelled the officer. Larry looked up with dull eyes. The man pointed to a different locker. "That one."

"Oh, yeah. Thanks," said Larry.

"I don't suppose you remember your combination?"

Larry grimaced. "I can hardly remember my name."

"I'm not surprised. You're an idiot, Klaus. How can you stay up half the night carousing and expect to function?" The man put the brush and boot on the floor, picked up a heavy fire extinguisher that was sitting in a corner, and walked over to Larry. Without a word he raised the extinguisher chest-high, and brought it down hard on the lock, which popped open and hung sadly from the door handle. "It's a good thing you're too cheap to buy a decent lock." He replaced the extinguisher and looked at his watch. "Twelve minutes."

Larry opened the door and gazed at the uniform. *His* uniform. It was beautiful. To the eyes and to the touch. Smooth gray with black collar and trim. Bright silver buttons. Black epaulettes, each sporting two silver stars. A half-dozen awards and decorations over the left breast pocket and SS insignia pins on both collar points. It was clean and perfectly pressed. And as Larry pulled it onto his body, a surge of power filled every corner of him. He felt strong. Important. Superior. The stripes on his arm said he was only a corporal, but no oriental potentate had ever felt more regal. All the garbage Yosef Jewboy had put him through had been worth it. The impossible dream had come true. "Thanks, Jewboy," he said.

"What?" asked the officer who was lacing up his glossy boots.

"Nothing. Talking to myself."

"Let's go."

"Right." Larry reached into the locker and took out his cap. Gray. Sleek black visor. And above the visor was something that made Larry's breath hitch. An embossed silver skull—the insignia of the Totenkopferbande. The Death's Head Brigade. The most feared division in the SS. If only those morons back home could see him now—his stupid teachers, the stupid judge, the stupid neighbors, his stupid lawyer, the legions of stupid people who looked at him like he was some lower life-form. As he put the cap on and pulled the brim down just above his eyes, a lump formed in his throat. No matter how long his life was destined to be, he would never again feel this good about himself.

"I'm going," his companion called, opening the barracks door.

"Right behind you."

The sun was warm and the sky cloudless. It would have been perfect but for a strange, nasty odor that Larry couldn't recognize. "Better than that Georgia hell-hole, anyway," he thought. As the two men strode toward Barracks 9, prisoners along the way dropped what they were doing, swept their caps off their heads, lowered their eyes, and stood at attention as the men

121

passed. "The way it oughta be," Larry said to himself. "Wonder what it would take for the Jew to let me stay here? Maybe he's already done it. Haven't heard from him for a while. Maybe he figures I'm better off here. Fine with me." Ramrod straight and proud, Larry and his comrade made their way across the camp, paying little or no attention to the ragged people around them. It was perfect. Except for the smell.

With only seconds to spare before the camp whistle blew signaling eight o'clock, the men stepped through the door of Barracks 9, into a small entryway. Even before the door closed behind him, Larry knew he was in a lab or hospital of some kind. The foul air of the outside was replaced by a somewhat less noxious mixture of alcohol, formaldehyde, and an assortment of other chemicals. Though he had no clue as to what he was supposed to do or how he was supposed to act, he was determined to pull off the charade. The art of the scam was always one of his long suits. Come what may, Larry Fishburn would always make it through.

"Here," his companion called, tossing Larry a white lab coat. "Check the boards."

"What?"

"THE BOARDS! THE BOARDS!" he yelled, pointing to the wall behind Larry. "What's the matter with you?"

Larry turned around and saw five clipboards hanging in a straight row. Above each was a name. Last name, first initial. He was Klaus Something-Or-Other. Only one of the names began with a K—Donneker, K. His name must be Klaus Donneker. He removed the clipboard under Donneker, K. and started reading his duty log for the day.

"What about mine?"

"Bluff time, " Larry thought, realizing he had yet to learn his associate's name. Without taking his eyes off his own paper, Larry blindly reached up and grabbed the first clipboard that came to hand. "Four to one odds," he thought. "Could be worse."

There was a long pause.

"Thanks," said P. Kolb, the name over the peg.

"Sometimes you get lucky," thought Larry, grinning.

They removed their SS tunics, donned the lab coats, and stepped through a doorway into a large ward room. P. Kolb glanced at Larry's duty sheet.

"J-Ward. You're right Klaus. You are lucky. Lucky you woke up too late for breakfast."

"Why?" Larry asked trying to mask the alarm in his voice.

P. Kolb ignored the question, and walked away scribbling on his clipboard.

The wards were clearly marked, and in alphabetical order. So it didn't take him long to find a door marked 'J-Ward:Juvenile Research.' His hand was on the knob when a chilling thought gripped him. What

if they should ask him to perform surgery or something? Could he fake his way out of that? Or what if
they asked him some technical question? Could he
fake his way through that? He clenched his teeth. Yes.
If he kept his wits about him he'd make it. He had to
make it. He was destined to be here.

As Larry's grip on the knob tightened, an incredible
but obvious fact entered his mind. D-Day was a year
away. What if he were to tell his superiors about it?
What if he were to tip them off, and they were able to
avoid the mistakes that had cost them the war? Larry
didn't know everything that had happened between
1943 and his own time, but he knew enough. Enough
to insure that Germany would win the war. Enough
to foretell computers and space travel and VCRs and
rock & roll years before they actually came to be.
Adolph Hitler would *make* history, because Larry
Fishburn had the power to *change* it.

The knob turned under his sweaty hand as
someone opened the ward door from the inside,
and Larry almost tumbled into the room. He saw a
lean, unsmiling man standing by a lab table, eyeing
him coldly. The man who had opened the door
scowled.

"You're late, Donneker," he snapped. "Again."

"Diplomacy," Larry thought. "Be cool."

"I'm very sorry gentlemen," he said, trying to muz-
zle his giddiness. "I wasn't feeling well."

"Was it a woman or a card game this time?" sniped the man at the table sarcastically. "Or both? Really, Corporal. You should be above such things. Do you think Hugo and I cavort around at all hours when there's important work to be done here?"

Hugo closed the door and said nothing. He loved watching Dr. Mannerheim dress down the SS men assigned to J-Ward, especially this poor excuse for a soldier. All spit and polish and no substance. Running roughshod over the Jews was about all they were good for. Death's Head Brigade? Dunder-Head Brigade was more like it.

"Bring in #411," Dr. Mannerheim directed.

"Right away, Doctor," answered Hugo who scurried into the next room like a mouse hunting for cheese.

"Now then, Corporal, do you think your addled brain could tolerate a review of this case?"

Larry nodded.

"You will recall that we're studying regeneration, particularly the regenerative capability of muscle tissue and bone over varying increments of time. We know that the human body can heal itself. But we don't know how or why or to what degree the healing happens. Our goal is to unlock this secret of nature. Once we understand the healing process, we can take steps to accelerate it. Imagine what our armies could do if we were to cut the recuperation time of our wounded men by a third or a half or more."

Hugo re-entered the room escorting a naked, ten year old child whose appearance made Larry step back. The boy was like something out of a horror movie. He could not have weighed more than forty pounds. Every bone was clearly visible, and bed-sores, many of them open and running, pock-marked his body. Most shocking to Larry was the boy's rickety gait. He tottered and lurched on his spindly, discolored legs like someone trying stilts for the first time.

Dr. Mannerheim's face lit up, his eyebrows rose, and a wide, warm smile spread across his features. "Come in, Avram," he exclaimed happily, "Come in. Come in. My, we're doing much better today, aren't we?"

The boy managed a wide-eyed, vacant smile and teetered over to the table. Dr. Mannerheim patted the boy's head.

"Look what I have for you, Avram" he said dipping his hand into his pocket and retrieving a dime-sized piece of chocolate. "Would you like this?" The boy managed a weak but unmistakable nod. "Well then, it will be waiting for you when you wake up. Let's get you up on the table. Corporal Donneker, will you help us please."

Larry couldn't move, unable to take his eyes off the skeletal figure. The doctor's friendly demeanor evapo-rated.

"DONNEKER! NOW!"

Startled, Larry moved haltingly to the table and helped Hugo lift the boy up and stretch him out on the steel tabletop. Touching him made Larry's skin crawl. The boy shivered violently as he was placed on the steel table..

"Yes, I know it's cold," Dr. Mannerhem said sympathetically with his friendly-mask firmly in place again. "I'll tell you what." He looked furtively around the room as if no one else were present, and leaned over the tiny figure. "If you're good," he whispered, and dipped into his pocket again, "two pieces of chocolate for my friend Avram. How would that be?" He gently patted the boy's head, and motioned to Hugo who was standing alongside the table holding a gauze mask and a bottle of ether. The mask was set on the boy's face, and within seconds, he was unconscious.

"All right, Hugo, that's enough. Let's begin."

Hugo set the mask and ether onto a counter, and pulled a pencil and small pad of paper from his coat pocket.

"#411," Dr. Mannerheim intoned, "male, Jewish, ten years of age. Session #5, April 17, 1943." He cleared his throat and looked at his assistant. "Getting all this?"

Hugo smiled. "Yes, Doctor."

"Good. Where was I? Ah, yes, session #5." He paused, collecting his thoughts, and continued his dictation. "Scar tissue regeneration is at perhaps fifty percent, in both legs and the bone regeneration significantly less than that, possibly as little as thirty percent, indicating that this should be the final session with this subject."

He paused briefly to let Hugo catch up. After a few seconds, Hugo, scribbling madly, looked up and nodded. The doctor continued.

"The patterns exhibited by #411 have thus far verified the data and conclusions outlined in my recent report, number 12A, and I have every reason to believe that the final stage will also bear out my findings... That's enough, Hugo. We'll do the rest later."

Larry found himself short of breath and fighting to keep his stomach down.

you're lucky you woke up too late for breakfast

"Corporal Donneker!"

When Larry didn't move, the doctor snarled and hurled a small rack of test tubes at him. The target was missed but the point was made.

"I'LL HAVE YOU SHOT IF YOU DON'T GET OVER HERE!!!"

"I can get through this," Larry thought as he moved to the table. "I can do it." His breathing became more and more shallow.

"I think the Totenkopferbande needs to reassess its recruitment policies," Hugo chortled.

"Quiet!" Mannerheim barked. He grabbed hold of Larry's coat and dragged him to the table. "Do your job, Corporal Donneker. Remember," he pointed to

the boy's twisted legs, "break the left femur inward, and the right one outward."

"Wha...?"

"Are you deaf as well as stupid?" He cupped his hands around his mouth and screamed into Larry's face, "HOW CAN WE TELL HOW A BONE MENDS IF WE DON'T BREAK THE BONE?"

Larry began to tremble. This had to be a dream. It had to be. His face turned the color of old parchment, sickly and sallow. Dr. Mannerheim wisely changed his approach..

"What's the problem, Corporal?" he asked calmly. "You've broken these same bones four times. And you've done your job well. Very well, I'd say. Why should this time be any different? Come on, man. You're SS. You're the elite. The Fuhrer's chosen people, so to speak. Don't disappoint us." He put a reassuring hand on Larry's shoulder. "Now, take a deep breath, and do what you have to do."

Larry turned back to the table and took hold of the child's thigh. It was so skinny he could nearly encircle it with his thumb and middle finger. He thought of his plans, of the money and prestige. Just a few foot/pounds of pressure to these already weakened bones. A couple of quick snaps. Like breaking twigs, really. Surely the promise of all that would be his was worth a couple of broken legs—Jewish legs.

velcro and vcrs, rockets and rock & roll

"For the Fatherland," urged Dr. Mannerheim softly. "And for science."

"For science?" Larry felt his voice rising uncontrollably. "FOR SCIENCE? YOU TWISTED PERVERT." He released the child's thigh, and moved deliberately toward the doctor who retreated until his back was against the wall. Larry grabbed him by the lapels, and repeatedly slammed him against the wall in a sickening rhythm.. "FOR SCIENCE? (slam) FOR SCIENCE? (slam) THIS IS MADNESS (slam)! MADNESS (slam)!! MADNESS (slam)!!!

Hugo scampered out of J-Ward, and by the time Larry let Dr. Mannheim's body drop to the floor, Hugo was well on his way to the commandant's office. Soon, he was tagging along behind a squad of SS, double-timing back to Barracks 9.

Larry knew they'd be coming for him. He bolted the door knowing it would hold the SS at bay for a few seconds at most. He turned around, ready to run to the rear of the building. Instead he stopped alongside the lab table. The boy, Avram, still unconscious, breathed heavily, and his body still shivered occasionally from the cold.

"I'm sorry," Larry whispered. He touched the boy's trembling hand. He couldn't stop the tears that welled up, blurring his vision. He didn't try. "I'm sorry. I'm really…" His throat tightened. No more words would pass. As he removed his lab coat and covered the little

131

boy, Larry's body began to shake violently, spasmodically. His head rocked back, and a long, terrible, tortured howl boiled up from within him, a scream full of awful pain and fear and anger. It emptied his lungs and froze the blood of the SS men massing in the corridor outside J-Ward.

He staggered from the table, gasping for breath, making his way to the rear of Barracks 9. He used a chair to smash an eye-level casement window and crawled out into the sunlight. He heard the soldiers, Klaus Donneker's comrades, running through and around the building, ready to blast their old friend to pieces.

And he heard the voice of Yosef Polanski.

"Why do you think they want to shoot you?" it said. "Because you assaulted the doctor, or because you wouldn't cripple the child?"

"Damn you!" Larry shrieked as he began a sprint to the electrified fence thirty yards away. Behind him someone yelled "Halt!"

Twenty yards.

"Klaus, stop!" It was the voice of P. Kolb.

Ten yards.

"Fire!" Bullets thumped into the dirt around his feet.

"DAMN YOU," cried Corporal Klaus Donneker, as he threw himself onto the fence. The blackness was instantaneous. There was nothing. But for the voice.

"Even yet, Mr. Fishburn. Even yet, you may not have seen the worst."

VII

It was as if someone had changed the channel. The fence, the soldiers, the camp—all vanished. Larry found himself sitting on a bench in a park, breathless.

Yosef Polanski was seated beside him.

The sun was bright and the birds sang summer songs. Larry heard the thumping of a basketball and the click of bicycle bearings. He knew the Jew was next to him, and he wanted to walk away. But he thought of a song he'd heard on the radio once. An oldie. Motown, most likely. *Nowhere to run to, nowhere to hide.*

"I've had enough," Larry said weakly. "Anyway you're wasting your time. What I am is what I am. You can't change that. Nobody can."

The scratchy voice he expected to hear in response was instead clear and resonant.

"May I tell you something, Mr. Fishburn? I came from a small village in Lithuania called Eishishok. I taught the children in a small school there. I remember teaching them one day about the yetzer hatov and the yetzer hara, the inclination to do good and inclination to do evil. 'All people are born with both,' I

133

told them, 'and it is up to the individual to decide which of the two impulses will govern his or her life.' My students were not impressed. They would not believe that Moses could have had a dark side. Nor could they believe that Hitler had anything but."

"I know what you're getting at. I'm telling you, I can't change anything."

Yosef Polanski turned to Larry.

"You refused to obey an evil order. You sacrificed much for a child who would die shortly, anyway. Why?"

"I don't know. Instinct. Besides what choice did I have? I was just riding around in the guy's body."

"Not so."

"What do you mean?" Larry asked, looking at the man's eyes for the first time. The Jew was still sickly pale, but his eyes were the saddest eyes Larry had ever seen.

"According to Dr. Mannerheim's records, Klaus Donneker obeyed every order given him without question or hesitation. Except during session #5. For some reason, not explained in the notes, he went berserk, assaulted Dr. Mannerheim, and was shot by security guards. No one knows why he acted as he did, not the Germans nor history."

Larry's eyes dropped to the grass by his feet.

"You did it, Mr. Fishburn."

"Instinct," he said.

"Yetzer hatov," replied Yosef Polanski.

"So now what? Where are we? When are we?"

"Near Los Angeles. And you are back in your own time. There is one more event you must witness." He pointed to a building across the street from where they sat.

"What is it?" Larry asked.

"A technical school. But today it is being used for a meeting which you will attend."

"And this meeting…this meeting is supposed to be worse than what I just went through?"

"Some would say."

"And when the meeting's finished…?"

"I too will be finished. I will not see you or speak to you again." He handed Larry an envelope. Inside was a bus ticket home and twenty dollars.

"Then let's get it over with," said Larry getting to his feet.

"But one day, *you* will see *me*."

Larry turned . "What's that supposed to…?"

Yosef Polanski was gone.

VIII

When he walked through the door, Larry saw that the lobby was filled with fifty or so milling people, people getting acquainted and reacquainted. The crowd was mostly male—lots of white shirts and ties. A short, round man walked over to Larry and extended his hand.

"Ned Carver, Pittsburgh. Glad you could make it."

"Larry Fishburn, Halliwell, Pennsylvania. It's near…"

"Near Philly, right? How do you like that? I've got family in Philly. Great town." He pumped Larry's hand enthusiastically, and clapped him on the shoulder. Larry smiled lamely, and scanned the crowd. What kind of horror could be lurking here? Were these guys closet devil worshippers or something? The whole thing looked like an Elks Club convention.

"Pretty great turnout, huh?" gushed Ned Carver.

"I don't know, this is my first time."

"Well, you've picked a f-a-a-a-ntastic meeting to come aboard. We've got people here from Canada, Germany, England…all over the place."

In a corner Larry saw a large placard perched on a tripod. The sign read:

WELCOME DELEGATES
TO THE ANNUAL CONVENTION OF
THE INSTITUTE FOR HISTORICAL REVIEW

"I must be in the wrong place," he thought. "Excuse me a second," he said to Ned Carver, and walked back out onto the sidewalk. He looked left and right. This was the only door in the only building on the block. Yosef Polanski could not have been pointing to anything else. Larry reentered the lobby and happily noted that Ned Carver was busy accosting someone else.

"I don't get it," he thought. "A convention of historians?"

A waiter walked by with a tray of pigs-in-blankets. Larry took three and swallowed them almost whole. He couldn't remember the last time he'd eaten. A large punchbowl was set up beside a long table across which were arranged dozens of books and pamphlets in neat, symmetrical rows. He tossed down one cup of punch at a gulp, and picked up a second. This one he drank more slowly, and as he did, he moved to the book table and scanned the titles. *The Six Million Jew Hoax, The Zionist Fraud, The Six Million Swindle, Did Six Million Really Die: The Truth At Last, The Hoax of the Twentieth Century, The End of a Myth: The Alleged Execution Gas Chambers at Auschwitz.* Larry looked back at the sign.

THE INSTITUTE FOR HISTORICAL REVIEW

What kind of institute was this? How come they had to meet here, instead of in their own headquarters? And how come there seemed to be only one topic under review?

"Hey, Lar." It was Ned Carver. "Thought I'd lost you. What do you think of all this?"

"I don't know. Could you answer something for me?"

"You bet."

"This Institute for…." He looked back at the sign.

"Historical Review," helped Ned.

"Right. Do they talk about anything except this stuff?" He gestured to the book table.

"Sometimes, sure. But for the most part exposing the so-called holocaust is what we're about. And why not? At a car dealers' convention they talk about cars. At a music convention they talk music. You wouldn't expect them to talk about anything else would ya?"

"No."

"So why should we?"

Larry couldn't follow the logic.

"So the whole point of your group is that the holocaust…"

"*Alleged* holocaust."

"Right. You believe that it never happened."

"It's a fact, Lar. There's not one shred of evidence to prove otherwise."

"But what about the photos and films?"

"Faked. Is there anything you *can't* fake on film?"

"And all the documents found after the war?"

"Forgeries."

"Written by…?"

"Jews, of course. See, they wanted to blackmail Germany to get the money they needed to start their own country. And what happened? Three years after the war ends, they get Israel."

"So you're saying that Israel was founded with money the Jews extorted from Germany?"

"Exactly."

"But after the war, Germany was bankrupt. They didn't have enough money to feed their own people. How could the Jews squeeze money from a country that was broke?"

"Listen, Lar, this is a very complicated issue. You need to do some serious reading and listen to the speakers we've got on the program today."

"Wait a second, I've got one more question."

"Okay, shoot."

"You're saying that Jews didn't die during the war?"

"No, no, Lar. Jews died in the war like everyone else. What we're saying is that there was no plan by the German government, in theory or in practice, that specifically called for the liquidation of the Jews."

"But what about the testimony of German soldiers after the war? They admitted…things."

"Sure they did. They were facing prison. To stay out, they told the judges what the courts wanted to hear. Foreigners were running the courts, remember."

"But since when do you try to stay out of jail by saying you're guilty? Especially if you're not. It doesn't make sense."

"It makes perfect sense. You confess, and you get a lighter sentence. It's plea bargaining and it happens all the time."

"But plea bargaining means saying you're guilty of a lesser charge, not mass murder."

"But there was no mass murder, Lar. Don't you get it? Anyone who says there was is either a Jew looking for sympathy or somebody looking to sell a book or get on *Geraldo*. Besides, who's left to say what happened fifty years ago? A handful of old geezers whose brains are getting soft with age. Get real. Their testimony wouldn't hold up under cross-examination. Any decent lawyer would cut them to pieces. We want the truth to come out."

"No you don't. You want your opinion to come out. You're supposed to get at truth by distilling from both sides of an issue. But you automatically reject any evidence or reasoning that doesn't jibe with what you want to believe."

Larry was aware that as his voice rose, the noise level in the lobby dropped to a murmur, and that more than a few heads were turned in his direction.

"You're just a bunch of bigots." He looked around at the crowd. He didn't yell, but his voice was strong and loud. "*We're all a bunch of bigots.* The only difference is I've got the guts to admit it. You clowns hide behind three-piece suits and phony organizations and pretend to give a damn about history. You couldn't care less about history. I may not be much, but I'm better than you because at least I'm honest about who I am. You're…the worst."

"Young man," said a voice. Larry looked and saw a tall, distinguished looking man walking toward him. Smiling. The man had silver hair and an almost regal bearing. A silk handkerchief protruded neatly from the breast pocket of his charcoal suit. Pinned to one lapel was a name tag that read "Hello. My name is ROLAND" "Young man," he said amiably. "Tell me one thing. Do you know anyone who was in any of the so-called death camps? Do you know anyone who actually witnessed these alleged atrocities? Or was a victim of them?"

Larry drew in a deep breath, and as he let it out sighed softly, "Yeah." He set his punch glass on the table and walked out.

IX

Halliwell never saw Larry Fishburn again. Judge Chalmers received Larry's paper via Federal Express the day before it was due, and Rabbi Szenes, after reading it and grading it 'Superior,' told Judge Chalmers that he would like to meet Larry.

But Larry was gone. No one knew where or why. His foster-parents initiated a half-hearted search, but, predictably, nothing came of it.

In Washington, D.C. some years later, an innocuous looking man standing in the line outside the Holocaust Memorial Museum turned his collar up against the February chill. He entered the museum and moved from exhibit to exhibit, eventually coming to a room of photographs. Dozens of pictures covering all four walls and extending upward tow ful stories. This, a sign read, was the Eishishok Collection, the wall of remembrance for a small Lithuanian village that was no more. The Jews had lived there for nine hundred years, and had grown to a population of 3,000, but it took only two days in September of 1941 for the Nazis, aided by local Lithuanian collaborators, to slaughter nearly the entire Jewish population. One child, Yaffa Eliach, survived to adulthood. He spent twelve years and searched three continents gathering and labelling these photographs that would document Jewish life in Eishishok. Families and lovers, friends and colleagues. Walking, bicycling, reading, playing, posing. Living. Those who were elderly and those who would never see old age. At work, at play, at study. A tiny civilization captured in two dimensions.

The man methodically scanned the wall, examining each face, until he came to a photo of a short, bearded teacher standing somberly behind nine equally unsmiling boys. The caption in the visitors' guide listed the names of the students. The teacher, however (nondescript but for a long scar running down the left side of his face), was unidentified. After staring at the picture for a long, long time, the man walked to an attendant and asked for a pencil and paper. He wrote briefly, folded the paper tightly, and handed it back to the attendant without a word.

"What's this?" asked the attendant.

"Nothing you'd understand," said the man as he walked away. "Just squaring the scales."